I0822407

DRAGON TEARS

A COMPANION NOVELLA TO

THE ALLIANCE OF THE DRAGON SWORD

※ ※ ※ ※

C. S. Johnson

Ebook ISBN: 978-1-948464-65-9
Hardback ISBN: 978-1-948464-66-6

Edited by Crystal McGough.

Crystal McGough is a freelance editor and stay-at-home mom with a bachelor's degree in Journalism. For more information, please email mcgoughcrystal@gmail.com.

For Sam, who helped me to see that there is some beauty that can only come from suffering—God's light shining through my tears have given my soul rainbows of the brightest hues.

This is also for all of my beloved supporters who helped make this book a reality:

Bryn Shutt
Tina Morley
David Willoughby
Chris Simpson
Jerilyn B.
Marty Hebert
Donna Swenson
Beth Cheatham
Rosemary Dewar
Natalia Netleson
Janice Ryberg
Lisa Tate
Sara Lawson
Evan Pokroy
Laura Pol
Natalia Ketelsen
Jeremy Reynolds
Ursula McClenny
Esther Kuzik
Robert Mesnard
Leslie Zak
Krissy Fee

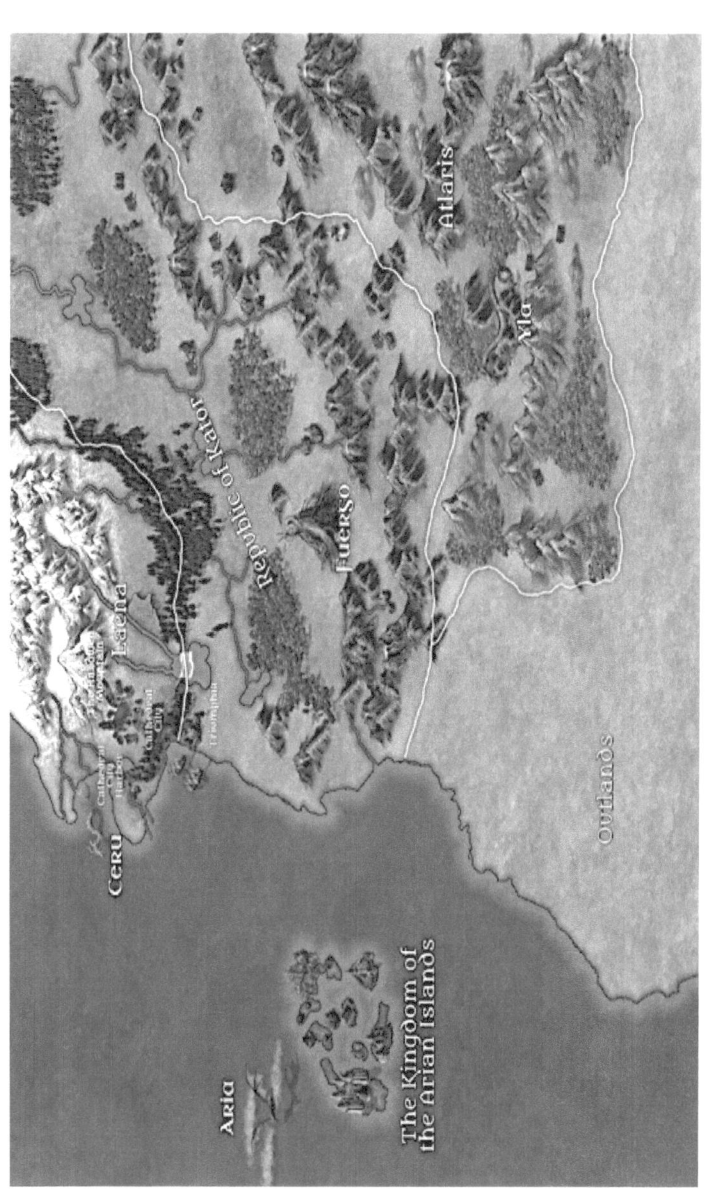

THE DRAGONLANDS

Prologue

※ ※ ※ ※

It was not supposed to be this way.

I blink back tears as I run, barely noticing the beauty of the snow-covered terrain around me. The sun is setting, but it is still light enough for me to find my way out of the mountain pass and head up toward the forest with ease. My once spotless boots slap hard against the powdered ground; each step I take away from my home slinks me further into the mud and muck of the earth. A kindred sense of devastation engulfs me, and I am tempted to weep for my once-spotless, fur-lined boots as much as my broken heart.

I breathe in and out, hard and fast, desperate not to scream as I sneak away; I can feel my eyes burn at both the chill in the air and the unshed tears I am desperately trying to hold back at the thought of leaving my home.

But I have no other choice; I can't stay.

Not after all that's happened to me.

My fingers are shaking along with the rest of my body as I scurry into the woods. The bag on my back swings with each step, urging me forward even as I face down my inner doubts.

My robe's hem catches on a hidden tree root, and I stumble forward, landing hard.

I bite down on my lip, stopping any yelp from escaping. I hold myself still for a long moment, before slowly letting my breath out; it is as if the world goes still along with me, and I need to make sure everything is in order before I allow any movement to resume.

As time reawakens, my hands sink further into the ground below; I can feel the warmth of mud on my dress.

And then I hear a small *chink*, and the world stops once more.

Dread pierces through me at the sight of the golden amulet laying on the ground.

Quickly and tenderly, I reach for it.

My fingers shake as I take hold of it and begin to untangle its golden chain. The charm captivates me, just like it always has; the gold is shaped in the form of a dragon, with its legs and tail curled around a singular sapphire gem. Ever since I first received it, I would look at it and see the Great Sea Serpent, Ceru. It wasn't a baseless assumption to do so, either; the amulet was known among the Laenite Tribe as The Crest of Ceru, and the golden features of the dragon's face carried the same long whiskers, as well as the same flared forehead.

Now, as I study it, I realize it isn't Ceru at all; there are no gills at the neck and no fins that branch out from its tail. The magic I'd felt before wanes and finally extinguishes itself.

No longer am I captivated—instead, I am crushed.

The sight of it sickens me as much as it once pleased me, and the depths of my humiliation and the darkness of my loneliness leave me momentarily breathless.

Ceru ... how could you do this to me? How could you deny me the only thing I'd ever asked of you?

My silent prayer cries out from the center of my being.

But it is all for naught.

I feel nothing; where there had been once warmth and certainty, there is nothing—and yet the emptiness I feel is so heavy and real, like a sea full of shadows, and I am drowning in its depths.

I am not sure what power it is that compels me to stand, but I do.

I put the amulet underneath my tunic and proceed to wipe myself off. The lapis blue and pristine white of my traveling gown are now splattered with muck and snow and even a smidge of spring's earliest grass. The warmth I'd felt after my fall is gone, cloaking me with an even more bitter cold.

It seems even the weather is mocking me, adding to the choir of other voices who have rejected me.

A sob chokes me as I stand there, and I am tempted to give up and return home.

"Thessa!"

My eyes widen in shock, and then narrow in anger.

Father Siah calls my name, the dying spark of my determination is lit anew.

I take off running again, this time faster than ever before.

He isn't coming for me. He's coming for the Crest.

As if in agreement, the golden pendant around my neck begins to hum. It pulsates against my chest, and even without looking, I can sense the power it holds. I press it further into my chest in silent defiance.

The Crest marked me as Ceru's Handmaiden, the one who tended to him directly—the one who was now set apart from the tribe and supposedly carried its future.

Ceru.

The design of the Crest is as mocking as the chill in the air. I used to curl up next to Ceru, just like the sapphire gemstone in the middle of the amulet.

My eyes sting as I think of the great beast who had adopted me.

As a younger child, I would sneak into his nest, as if to dare myself to look at him and be afraid.

And I was afraid—at first. But then Ceru spoke to me, and I adored him almost immediately. He was still a fierce beast, with his long, dragon body, with his large, flared fins and the scales which would occasionally fall from his body. But he was also gentle—with a tenderness I didn't believe possible, he would nuzzle my cheek and press his forehead against mine, and all my fear would disappear.

My childhood was dotted with nights where I would creep down the stairs from the orphanage corridor in the Hallowed Mountain and seek him out. Sometimes he would sleep, and other times, he would talk with me, all while the other priests and attendants were away. He seemed to appreciate the company, and he never turned me away. I would eventually drift off to sleep. The following mornings, I would wake up and find Ceru's long tail protectively sheltering me.

Later, when I was twelve, Ceru did something no one had seen in years; he cried out a dragon tear for me when Davar, one of my friends, suffered from a broken leg. Ceru's tears had the power to heal, and after witnessing Davar's complete, instant recovery, the High Priests and Spiritual Mothers were quick to request more, and soon I was retrieving dragon tears at their behest.

So when Ceru gave me Crest two years before—against the wishes of the High Priest—I never thought it was strange I would receive it.

But then, I never thought I would hate it, either.

The Crest had been passed down in the Laenite community since our patriarch, Laen, came to the northern continent—now known as Laena—and settled here, his family in service to Ceru, the Great Sea Serpent and Water Dragon, the Guardian of the Laenite Tribe.

After Laen had proclaimed his allegiance to Ceru all those centuries ago, Ceru had gifted Laen with the Crest. It was a talisman made of the brightest gold and a small gemstone, and it was rumored those who carried it were deemed worthy to carry special blessings.

While there had been reservations in giving the Crest to me, I have always carried it with me.

And yet, despite everything, today is no exception.

"Thessa! Thessa, where are you?"

Father Siah is not giving up.

I keep moving forward, but I slow down, trying to keep silent. The temptation to glance back grows suddenly and exponentially.

Had I not been so irrevocably lost already, I might have given in, looked back, and given up. I might have even allowed Father Siah to catch up with me and escort me to go back home.

But it is not my home anymore. After Garrison's departure, there is nothing left in all of Laena for me now.

Nothing, and no one.

Not even Father Siah.

"Thessa, please," Father Siah calls again. "Thessa?"

There's a sense of exasperation in his words, but I know he is worried, too. He is not supposed to show me any favor over the others living in the Hallowed Mountain, even though I was assigned to his care as a baby and he has always been the closest thing I had to an actual father.

That is likely why he is the one searching for me; Father Ephyras, the High Priest of Cathedral City, would've known if I would listen to anyone, it would be Father Siah.

Anger burns through me all over again at the thought of the High Priest.

I will not miss Father Ephyras. After Ceru, I place the blame for my current pain and sorrow squarely at his feet. Two years had passed since Ceru had given me the Crest, and in that time, rarely had a day passed that Father Ephyras didn't chide me for something, no matter how inconsequential. He thought I was underserving of such an honor.

For a dark moment, as I listen to Father Siah call for me again, I almost want to agree with him if it means being spared all the pain I feel.

"Thessa, I know you're upset." Father Siah sounds winded now, in addition to worried. "But I need you to come back. Your community needs you now more than ever."

Quickly, I press my hand over my mouth, torn between laughter and tears.

Why would they need me?

True, I worked as a healer for my assignments, tending to many of my countrymen's ills, and sometimes giving Ceru's tears to my patients.

Will they be able to continue caring for the sick and the injured without me?

At once, I shake my head, determined not to feel guilty. But Father Siah was right; my absence would create more pain for others. Familiar faces of those I'd treated over the years come to the forefront of my mind, and I squeeze my eyes shut, desperate to keep them away.

Why should I care for their suffering? They never cared for mine!

My community had watched me suffer my entire life—assuming they were watching me at all—and they were the ones who caused much of my suffering with their derision and belittlement. Despite my high status as Ceru's Handmaiden, I was still without a family and, as a result, I lacked a proper place in their society.

It was tragically laughable to think they needed me at all, especially after the last week.

They don't need me, and I don't need them.

I swallow hard at the thought, wishing I could truly believe it.

The Laenites are my bloodline; they have watched over the snowy mountains since the Era of the Dragons began fourteen generations ago, when the Creator sent them to us, and the tribes, tongues, and nations have now settled around them in clusters of civilization. Family and religion was at the heart of all we did, so much so that Cathedral City was built to be an extension of the heart of the Hallowed Mountain.

What I lacked in family, I made up for with religion. The Creator was a gracious God, who brought about life and all its beauty; but the humans rebelled, and learned that they would suffer as a result. The Dragonlands were his blessed nation, although we were fractured because of the different Guardians and their charges. It never occurred to me that we weren't all part of the same nation, the same beginnings, and the same ending. With Ceru as my only example, I saw the Dragon Guardians as good, kind, and well-meaning, even if Ceru's power seemed limited. One day, the Creator promised to unite us, but only after the Age of Dragons had passed.

Despite that, though, I still felt lonely and abandoned. I didn't know much about my parents, having been adopted, other than I was born of the blood and water of Ceru's people. While I willingly and eagerly accepted the Hallowed Mountain as my home, like anyone without a real family, I longed for one more than anything else.

I don't have to look back on the mountain now to see the peak of it thrusting into the clouds, making it seem as though the world had folded over onto itself, making a symmetrical land, where the snow and rock of the mountain would bleed into clouds and sky.

Before today, I might've stopped and lingered, overwhelmed by the beauty before me. Under the mountain, I know there is a spring of the purest water, and that is where Ceru, the Great Sea Serpent and the Water Dragon, makes his home with me and the others who serve him.

"Father Siah? Did you find Thessa?"

My heart skips a beat at the sound of Philia's voice. She and her twin sister, Pia, are my best friends, the closest thing I have to real sisters, and fate sticks another knife in my chest as I realize I am leaving them, too.

"No, not yet," Father Siah answers with resolved sadness. I am close enough to hear them speak, but still hidden enough that they don't see me. "Do you have any idea of where she might go?"

I can almost see Philia bite her lower lip, anxious and indecisive. I pause in my steps, slipping into the shadows of a large tree, waiting for her answer. There is a small collection of snow-covered bushes around it, and I know I am small enough I can hide as long as I am careful to cover up the blue of my robes. Philia knows me well—perhaps too well—but surely even she wouldn't have an inkling of my plans.

"I know Thessa was upset about Garrison," Philia finally says. "If I had to guess where she'd go, I'd say she'll try to meet up with him in the Arian Islands."

Father Siah groans. "Why would she go and see him, though? He's the one—"

"Because she loves him!" Philia interrupts him sternly. "She's never loved anyone like him, Father."

I love how Philia scolds him. Father Siah was the one who knew me best throughout my life, but he never realized how much I'd grown up since becoming Ceru's handmaiden and meeting Garrison.

If he found me, Father Siah would likely treat me as though I were still a child; he would put a hand on my shoulder, not gentle enough to show his favor, but strong enough so that I could sense it—and then he would likely guilt me into returning to Cathedral City.

"Oh, Thessa," he would murmur, before tucking the stray tresses of my long, blond hair behind my ear. "These things will pass."

That was his standard advice—and this time, we both knew he would be wrong.

Just like he was wrong about Garrison.

Father Siah lets out a small curse, shocking me and Philia.

"Father!" Philia murmurs, horrified.

"Forgive me," he replies bitterly. "But this is unprecedented. We need to find her, Philia. She carries the hope of all of Laena with her."

Philia steps closer to him and bows her head reverently. "I know you love her very much, Father. You must not give up your hope. We must believe we will see her again."

"No, you won't, if I have anything to say about it," I whisper softly. Even though they can't see me, I give both of them a bow, and then I slip away again, heading into the forest.

I have to keep one hand over my mouth as I run, moving away as quickly and quietly as possible. I am grateful for the physical demands of my journey, even if they are difficult and tiresome. After all the years working with Ceru's medical healers, I know mourning is a necessity, but it is just as often a luxury.

And right now, it is one I don't have.

Father Siah's voice fades, along with Philia's, and others' voices who call my name behind me.

Long moments pass and stretch out as I stumble along the path. Every step takes me further away from home and further into darkness.

Soon, I only hear the sound of my heart pounding inside my chest and the large huffs of my tearful breaths. There is an extra bite to the wind now that the sun is gone, the moon is rising, and clouds are gathering in great bunches.

A rumble of thunder crashes through the night; at the sudden sound, I stumble again. This time, I feel a rocky sharpness slice into my flesh.

"Ouch," I whimper bitterly, struggling to hold in my complaints as I rub my leg. At the cut of cold air across my knee, I know I've drawn blood, even if it's too dark to see it.

I put my head in my hands and allow myself a moment to steady myself—just for a moment. I know my tears won't come; stopping now is only forcing me to suffer more.

No one had seen me leave the mountain fortress, and even if they did, I had enough of a head start I would still be able to reach the Great Waterfall at the southern edge of Laena.

"Why, Ceru?" My words are muffled by my hands, but I know he can hear me. "Why did you do this to me?"

Garrison's handsome face comes to the forefront of my mind. I see his eyes, sharp and kind, their gray-green complementing a clear and perfect day; I can almost feel the softness of his dark blond hair and recall the smoothness of his cheeks. His lips are curled in an irresistible, surly smirk, and I cry harder, remembering how it felt to have them pressed against my own in a passionate kiss.

Why, Ceru?

Inside my heart, a treacherous whisper says it wasn't Ceru who had caused my pain, but my mind couldn't bear to think the only man I'd ever loved was the one truly responsible for my current heartache.

I'm not sure how much time passed before I look up, inhale sharply, and let out a long, shaky breath. I push back all the pain I feel and shove aside all the blame.

For so long, I'd believed we as humans had no recourse against the stream of fate and its master. In serving Ceru all my life, I had never questioned that idea.

And that is why I am here, running away.

That is why I am alone, humiliated, and rejected, despite my long years of work and service, diligence, and obedience, not to mention my love and trust.

The Crest bumps against my breast again, but this time I ignore it.

The ground is as hard and cool as my resolve as I push myself up and stand once more.

It is time to move on.

I press back my hair as another bolt of lightning flashes, letting the light catch on the dark golden locks. I pull my cloak more tightly around me, and I continue forward.

Ahead of me, tucked along the cliffs that line the southern end of Laena's main island, is the Great Waterfall. While Laena is home to several waterfalls, there is only one that marks the end of Laena's border and Ceru's protection, and I am determined to make it there.

I look up to the sky, despaired to see the stars covered by the rainclouds. With the weather like this, it will be a three-day journey at least, one that requires running through different woods, climbing up rocky terrain, and walking along frozen fjords.

But I *will* make it to the waterfall, I tell myself.

Another bolt of lightning streaks across the sky, and thunder crackles in angry waves.

I swallow hard, but stand firm. *It is time to determine my own fate.*

But even as I fortify my determination, everything that has happened to bring me to this place calls back to me; the memories, the people, and Ceru, and Garrison …

I take one step after another, as the past bleeds into my present and takes me back two years before, back to the days when I loved Ceru without doubt, when I first met Garrison, and when my heart was still unbroken. The memories, as joyous as they were to make, are now bitter, and my only comfort comes from knowing the Great Waterfall is waiting for me at the end of my path.

CHAPTER ONE

※ ※ ※ ※

Two Years Earlier …

No one ever paid attention to a Ghost.

By the time I was twelve, I was used to how often eyes slid over me and the others as we went about our work. We were considered an essential, if regrettable, part of life in Laena, but as odd as that may sound, that was just how things were. In many ways, it was an understandable situation, too.

The Ghost Children of the Laenite Tribe were children who were born out of wedlock, orphaned at a young age, or even on the rare occasion, abandoned by our parents. The "Ghost" moniker was rumored to have been a jest originally, but as we were the remnants of incomplete lives, forgotten dreams, or abandoned mistakes, it was a label that carried a cruel truth.

In our community, where faith came first and family came second, Ghost Children were largely an afterthought.

However, the others and I did not allow this to be a point of contention between us and other Laenites. It wasn't as though the world and its realities left us unprepared. The Creator had given us a beautiful place to live and thrive, but because of sin, darkness, and despair, imperfections and abuses, there was an endless, growing chasm between humanity and divinity—all of this was unable to be ignored or denied. Our religion taught us to embrace our positions as the invisible shadows of our society, and through our work, even if it was not acknowledged, we kept the light burning ever more brightly.

To us, this was only right, since we were the adopted children of Ceru, the Great Sea Serpent and the Water Dragon Guardian of Laena.

Like the other Ghosts, Ceru took me in as an abandoned baby and gave me a bed, clothes, food, and a traditional education. It was thanks to Ceru that I had grown up surrounded by the hills of my home, where snowy mountains bled into waterfalls like open wounds and flowers dotted the ravines all throughout spring.

The arrangement had a sacred name in the ancient tongue, but the Laenites often referred to it as a Life Debt. Ceru saved my life when he adopted me, so it was my duty to serve and honor him.

Since I was a baby when my parents left me, I would be released from my Life Debt in my seventeenth year; if he'd saved my life as a grown adult, I would have been honor-bound to serve him for seven years or until he released me from my debt.

On my fourteenth Adoption Day—a Ghost Child's equivalent of a birthday—I received my main job assignment with the medic healers of Cathedral City. One year had passed since then, and ever since I started, I had enjoyed learning all I could about tending to different wounds and injuries, caring dutifully to the last moments of a dying life, and educating my patients on their recovery needs and expectations. Much like how I'd been drawn to Ceru's underground nest, I felt drawn toward my work as a healer.

Even when we lost a community member to disease or old age, I was greatly comforted by Ceru's assurance that such souls had entered into a better place; it was said the Dragon of Death would carry faithful souls to the Eternal Hall of the Creator, where we would live in endless joy. In this way, our grief was not without hope, and even in our sadness, I still found a gleam of goodness.

By far my favorite part of the job was helping the new mothers. I envied them the most, despite their obvious discomfort and their childbearing pain. The babies I helped birth made my heart flutter and ache at the same time, and while I had no husband to marry or admirer to court, I imagined falling in love wasn't so different from how I felt seeing that first glimpse of new, created life.

Each time I handed a mother her new baby, I felt a spark of fulfillment as much as a twang of longing.

I was grateful for what I had been given, I truly was; but as much as I loved Ceru and my home, my job, and my friends, I desperately wanted a family of my own.

There was something so alluring about the thought of running my own household, having a husband coming home to my hugs and kisses, and adding children to the world who were born out of the mutual adoration in my marriage.

It was so easy to picture that perfection inside my mind, even if I didn't have any idea what my future husband would look like.

Still, that only added to some of the mysterious allure. One day my husband could be tall and tan, with a large frame and soft eyes; the next he could have long hair and dimples that hugged his smiles. I didn't mind if he was long and lanky, or if he was short and stocky; as long as he loved me, I would love him more than anything else in the world, and we would never be happy unless we were together.

"Thessa! What are you doing?"

At the sound of Mother Nia's voice, I blinked, and my daydreams blurred into the scene before me, where I was tending to a sleeping patient. I was using a damp cloth to cool down a man's feverish brow, but I'd been caught up in thinking of tending to my own children in such a loving manner that I'd failed to notice the water was being so thickly applied, it was soaking his pillow.

"Oh." I quickly stepped away and gave Mother Nia a sheepish look.

"You're going to drown him if you're not careful." Her mouth was firmly set, but her ancient eyes lit up with a hidden laugh as she moved to adjust her habit.

"Well, it wouldn't be the worst thing to happen to him today," I replied with a joking smile.

Mother Nia clicked her tongue. "Impertinent girl," she murmured, but I saw her struggle to compose herself; I counted my retort as a win when she turned away from me.

From across the room, another voice spoke up in scolding tones. "If you ask me, Thessa's too distracted to work tonight."

I glared over at Kana, not surprised to see the disapproval on her otherwise perfect face. Kana was another Ghost who worked with me in the healer station. She was a little younger than me by a few months, but despite our similarities, I knew we would never be friends. We got along out of ritualistic necessity, even when I could see the underlying hints of her animosity.

Times like this.

"Forgive me, Mother Nia," I replied dutifully, lowering my eyes until I was absolved for my inattention.

No one ever paid attention to a Ghost—not unless we were doing something wrong. In my case, it did not help that Kana was quick to point out my shortcomings.

"Yes, yes, child." Mother Nia's normal reserved expression had returned by the time she waved away my meaningless apology.

"Now, hurry. The pillow needs to be changed out quickly. We don't want Zebedee to get a cold."

"I will." I shot Kana a determined look.

"Perhaps I should take over for her tonight," Kana offered. "It is Thessa's Adoption Day, after all."

"That's true," I said, keeping my tone agreeable but not affirming. "But I can still work. My meeting with Father Ephyras isn't for another hour at least."

Kana held steady. "But if you're endangering the patients—"

"I'm sure Thessa won't let it happen again," Mother Nia said with a small, labored sigh. "And she's hardly endangering Zebedee, Kana. Honestly, if a man his age can survive falling into a ravine during combat drills, I'm sure a little extra water won't bother him. Now, be silent, girls, and get back to the tasks you've been assigned."

Mother Nia's face wrinkled as she gave us a warning glance and then shuffled out of the room.

Kana sneered at me before she went back to changing the bedsheets of another empty cot.

I felt heavy-hearted as Kana ignored me. I wasn't sure why we always seemed to have such trouble between us.

Kana was well-known for her good looks and intelligence. She had a larger group of friends than I did, and despite the rule of forbidden favorites, many of the priests and nuns around Cathedral City gushed over her more often than not.

Pia once told me that Kana hated being younger than me, and while I thought that was just silly, it was technically the one thing she would never accomplish over me—she could easily do a better job with our studies and accomplish more in the medical station. When it came to looking the part, Kana was organized, put-together, and always on time. I was always running a little late, my robes were a little wrinkled from sleeping in Ceru's mountain nest, and cleaning my room was a chore and a half.

"Did I hear that girl right? It's your Adoption Day?"

Zebedee stirred in his bed, and as I turned to face him, I saw him looking up at me with wonder.

"Yes, sir." I was glad he was awake; I wouldn't have to work as hard to get the pillow out from underneath him. "I'll be headed to the Cathedral after I'm done here."

"You should go then." Zebedee gave me a half-smile, one that looked painful from underneath the thick bandage on his head. "It's your fifteenth year, isn't it? Some young man will surely be ecstatic to have you as his bride."

Since we had been friendly for months, I gave Zebedee a quick kiss on the cheek. "I'm sure I can make an old man happy that I'm his medic."

Kana let out a discreet cough, and without looking, I knew she was rolling her eyes at me as Zebedee laughed.

"I'm surprised you're feeling so well. Especially since you had a rough tumble," I said. "Your first commander was horrified by the sight of you falling off the rocks."

"Ah, well … I should've been expecting it," Zebedee said. "Ceru's getting old, too, Thessa. His city and Laena itself are starting to crumble."

I felt a lump in my throat. The High Priests taught us through their records of history and prophecies that one day, the Age of Dragons would be over, and a new order would begin through bloodshed and sacrifice.

There was not much I doubted Ceru could handle—but the word of the Creator was not to be ignored, either.

But surely, I told myself, there were times when it was best to ignore such theories? Ceru, while he was old, had me and the other Ghosts by his side. We loved him, and I knew we would continue taking care of him for many years to come.

On the other hand, Zebedee was an old man, and perhaps he was just trying to massage his own ego by saying the main island of Laena was starting to weaken.

"Now, now," I said calmly, "Saying such things won't push Ceru to love you any more than he already does. I'm sure you'll get a dragon tear if he hears you need it."

"I doubt I'll need it. Ceru likely needs them more than I do, the way things are looking," Zebedee said, grimacing with pain. "But I'll take some painkillers if you have them ready."

I did my best to brush off his concern for Ceru. Zebedee was an older man, and stubborn, too. I wouldn't be able to convince him Ceru was fine, no matter how long I spent arguing with him.

But if nothing else, Zebedee was right. Painkillers would help. "I'll go and retrieve them for you."

Zebedee nodded. "After that, promise me you'll go and see Father Ephyras. I know you're eager to have your marriage arranged, but the community wants to hear who the very lucky man will be just as much as you do."

"All right." My cheeks flushed over with humbled pleasure, even if I doubted he was correct on that point, too. "Thank you, Zebedee."

True to my word, I finished my last chore for the night and headed out. Even Mother Nia seemed glad Zebedee had gotten me to agree to leave early. Both of them offered their blessings as I left, and the memory of their quiet, sincere affection kept me warm as I moved through the streets of Cathedral City.

A few others waved at me, and I waved back, surprised by the attention.

Maybe Zebedee wasn't entirely incorrect.

I was still a Ghost, but now that I was fifteen, and it was my Adoption Day, I was starting to become more of a real person in the eyes of the community.

The sun was still high enough in the sky I could see clearly all the way to the top of the Hallowed Mountain. As I walked down from the medic station, I sighed contentedly at the sights before me.

The market in the city was bustling with a lively energy, like the invisible echoes of a song, and its rhythm was one with the beat of my own heart.

The Cathedral of the Great Sea Serpent was a massive building, built at the bottom of the Hallowed Mountain, where Ceru resided and labyrinthian springs of water kept him connected to the rest of the world. On either side of the mountain, a crescent arm of land curled around, making a natural harbor, where community members would keep their fishing ships and other seacraft. Behind the mountain, there was the forest of Laena, with its various trails, and then even further back, there was mostly farmland where the people of Laena peacefully resided. There were some other mountains, too, and then at the back of the island, there was the Great Waterfall of Laena. It was at the opposite end of the island from the

Cathedral, running down the middle of the island's natural plateau.

At the bottom of the waterfall was marked the border between us and the home of Fuergo, the Fire Dragon Republic of Kator. They filled in a large chunk of the rest of the main continent, though there were several ongoing border disputes and historical claims with the Earth Dragon, Yla, and her nation, Atlaris, or so I'd heard.

The leaders of the Laenite Tribe had long ago decided not to interfere with the affairs of the world, and it was precisely because of Yla and Fuergo's various forms of warfare that history could attest to the wisdom of that decision.

"Thessa, there you are! Good heavens, did you hear?"

I barely had time to prepare myself before I found Philia rushing into me. She embraced me in a quick, sisterly hug, which I tried to reciprocate before she began jumping up and down.

"What is it?" I asked, laughing at her wild enthusiasm before catching some myself. "Did you hear something about me for my Adoption Day?"

"Oh, that's right. That's today, too." Philia's pretty face ducked down in apologetic shame. "I forgot."

"There's no issue," I assured her, even though I felt a little disappointed. I hid my hurt from her and gripped her hands with some measure of excitement. "Tell me what's happening."

"Oh, Thessa, an Arian ship is pulling into the harbor." Philia grinned. "And it's a big one, too. Perhaps we will get to hear another concert, maybe? What do you think?"

"I don't know," I admitted, although I was intrigued.

The Arian Islands were our neighbors from across the Western Seas. They served under Aria, the Dragon of Air, and their kingdom was made on artificially connected islands. They were full of talented artists and musicians, known for their appreciation and desire for beauty throughout the rest of the world. Occasionally, they would visit other regions of the world to showcase their talents or expand their trade routes.

"Come and see," Philia said, tugging on my hands. "They should be at port in a few moments."

I hesitated only for a moment; I wanted to go to the Hallowed Mountain, back to where Father Siah and the High Priest would be waiting for me, along with a message from Ceru regarding my Adoption Day—a message which possibly would inform me of who I was to marry after my Life Debt was over.

But Philia kept pulling on me, and after I took a look at the water clock set up in front of the Cathedral, I saw I had a little time to indulge my friend.

"Come on, Thessa," Philia insisted. "Pia's already down there, and Davar and Edmun are headed that way, too. They were told to report there for their soldier training in full uniform, so you know it has to be something important."

"They were?" I began walking with Philia, watching as she bubbled over with pleasure. She was a little over a year younger than me, and I couldn't help but feel old as she tried to hold my hand and skip down the street.

"Oh, yeah," Philia said. "Pia's already down there because of her job, but she'll be let out by the time we get there. And I was let out of work early today since one of the younglings spit up on me."

"Ew." I shook her off my arm. "You should've told me that earlier."

"I was wearing an apron." Philia nearly doubled over in laughter as I let out a silent prayer of thanks that I'd been appointed to work with the healers.

My friends and fellow Ghosts were old enough that each had been assigned a job, but I loved mine the most. Philia worked with the younger children as an assistant teacher; she would be promoted to a primary teacher in a few more years, and then she would work until she was married. Pia, her twin sister, worked down by Cathedral City's main port, overseeing fisherman and food production. I still saw them frequently, despite my longer shifts, but it was harder to keep up with my friends Davar and Edmun, since in addition to their jobs, boys were called to train as part of the Laenite Tribe's armed forces, but when we had a chance to meet, we did. As much as it interrupted my Adoption Day, I smiled at the thought of seeing them again.

"Ooh, Thessa, remember last time the Arians came? They brought us spools of fine cloth and those lovely shoes," Philia gushed. "And that jewelry, too!"

"You know Ghosts like us aren't supposed to draw attention to ourselves," I reminded her. "Why get so excited?"

"I'm more excited for you," Philia said. "Your Adoption Day is today. Surely, you'll get your marriage arranged, and as a bride, you can be as extravagant as you'd like."

As we made our way down to the port, Philia continued to babble, filling my head with even more daydreams and ideas. I couldn't help but allow her ideas to whisk my imagination away into another world, and even the sight of the Arian ship tying off into port couldn't fully bring me back to attention.

"Philia, Thessa, over here!"

Over the gathering crowds, I heard Davar calling out to us from the adjacent dock. I could see the dark burgundy of his hair sticking out from his helm. Philia had been right, it seemed; Davar was in his full armor, decked out in his gilded breastplate and the formal, silver-embroidered leather underneath his chainmail.

We made our way over to the adjacent dock as the Arian ship crept closer to shore.

"Where's Edmun?" I asked as we approached.

"He went to go with some of the other Ghosts," Davar said. "Father Piet ordered him to get Cathedral City's best guesthouses ready."

"So you know who's coming? What have you heard?" Philia asked Davar as we greeted each other.

"You wouldn't believe me if I told you." Davar straightened with pride, clearly enjoying having the upper hand over us; it was a rare occasion. "I've heard some of the port keepers talking about it."

"Well, tell us, then," Philia insisted. "Don't be cruel and make us wait. Is it another concert tour?"

"No, and praise the Creator for that." Davar stuck out his tongue in light disgust. He had no patience for music, although I had to wonder if that was intentional. Thanks to Philia, who often took to gossiping, we knew that Davar's father had likely been an Arian singer.

"Word has it that the Arian king has sent his highest-ranking ambassador here, and the ship's marking proves it," Davar said. He pointed toward the mast, where a royal purple flag waved in the breeze. "See the silver design on it? That's the coat of arms for the Rico family."

"It's so elegant," Philia said with a happy sigh. "I wonder what they've brought us? Maybe a new flag for Cathedral City's public square? That would be lovely. Father Dion was just mentioning about seeing to the City's upgrades."

"I don't know," I said, suddenly noticing the small legion of troops standing on the top deck. "They've come with soldiers."

"Well, I doubt it's an invasion if you're worried about that. They wouldn't be that foolish," Philia said. "Laena is very self-sufficient, and that's largely because our troops help protect us."

Davar grinned. "Of course we do, so you're welcome."

"Who says I was talking about you?" Philia teased. "You're still at a minor rank."

"Still better than you," Davar snapped back.

"Well, it's not my fault that women don't fight, is it?"

"Women like you are the reason we fight. We protect the rest of the world from having to deal with the likes of you."

I bit back a sigh as I ignored them. Philia and Davar had always been close, and with each passing year, I often wondered if they fought to prove they weren't secretly in love. Due to the mysterious nature of their heritage, Ghost Children were not often allowed to marry each other. Ceru would be the one who would have the final say in that matter, but given the odds, I couldn't blame Philia and Davar for their squabbles. Smaller pains in the present helped to possibly avoid larger ones in the future.

That was part of the reason the Laenites did not encourage some of the courting rituals many of the other countries and nations had, too. From what I knew of other nations' temporal relationships, divorces, and dating disasters, I was honestly relieved. I wanted a lasting love, a love that I could rely on to strengthen and support me; something I could add to and something that could give back something even more beautiful.

As Davar and Philia continued to tease and taunt each other, I kept my eyes on the approaching ship. It was a grand one, with silk-lined sails and intricate carvings along both sides. The Arians were known for their spectacle as much as their presentation.

I squinted as I saw a soldier moving across the ship, headed for the point of the bow.

The sun's setting light flickered over his helmed brow like a kiss of lightning. I watched, intrigued, as he took out a small flute and began to play.

The trill of the music fluttered down from on high in a lovely wave, making my heart lurch inside my chest.

I had always adored music. Both in my darkest midnights and my bright moments of joy, I would sing songs and find strength and sustenance.

I looked for the source of the song, and found myself staring at a man near the maidenhead of the ship.

The flute player held himself upright with confidence and flare, and as I watched him play, I almost wished I'd learned how to play an instrument, too. I was part of the worship choir as a singer, but I had no great talent.

I decided right then and there that if I ever had the time, I would write Ceru a song I could sing while another played the flute.

"Oh, that's beautiful." Philia leaned against my shoulder as she finally took notice of the music.

"Please, he's not that good," Davar argued, which sparked another argument with Philia.

I heard another shout from behind the flute player, and the music halted in mid-song.

A breath of stillness and silence took over.

And then, in the blink of an eye, the Arian boat suddenly slammed against the receiving dock.

The dock's wooden titles snapped. Ropes alternatively tightened and lagged, while several others called out everything from orders to screams of horror.

My eyes widened in shock as I watched the flute player. He wobbled dangerously atop the maidenhead of the ship, and just like before, a long, seemingly endless moment passed as we watched, transfixed by the danger.

And then fate finally gave its verdict.

Philia gasped, and even Davar's mouth dropped open as the flute player lost his battle with his balance, and he fell forward off the ship.

I closed my eyes as he met the water's surface in a devastating *splash*.

CHAPTER TWO

※ ※ ※ ※

"Somebody help!"

Everything seemed to happen at once. The Arian captain peeked over the side of the ship, crying out for his men to throw down a rope as the flute player floundered in the harbor.

The fallen young man wasn't able to grab the lowered rope before he sank deep below the surface.

"What's wrong?" Philia cried. "Can't he swim?"

"It's his armor," Davar explained, stepping in front of Philia and trying to shield her from the sight. "Even though the water's not that deep, he won't be able to swim to the surface unless he's able to get all his armor off or they can rescue him."

I looked to the captain, only to see the grim look on his face. Nearby, two smaller fisherman were paddling their boats over toward the ship in hopes of helping, but there was no way they would make it in time.

Something has to be done.

Glancing around again, I saw a spool of rope nearby.

At once, I had an idea.

"Davar, get that rope for me," I ordered, pointing to a supply pile just off to our left side. "Philia, help me out of my outer robes. Quickly, we don't have much time!"

The two of them were clearly still upset by the scene, but they listened to me without hesitation. I threw off my blue-colored robe and tied Davar's rope around my waist. As I secured it with a second knot, I realized there was a sudden blush on Davar's face as he saw me. The underlayer of my outfit still covered my torso, but without the outer robe, my arms and lower legs were exposed.

Normally, I would've laughed at his embarrassment—but right now, I had to focus on getting to the flute player before he drowned.

I would have to worry about Father Ephyras chastising me for my impropriety later.

"When I get to him, wait until I tug on the rope, and then pull us in," I instructed them.

Philia tightened her grip my robe. “But Thessa—”

“No time,” I shouted, already running toward the end of the dock. Once I reached the edge, I leaped off and plunged forward into the water.

Water rushed at me, washing away the cries calling out from the dock and the port, including Philia and Davar’s voices. Other boats all seemed too far away to help.

“Go, Ghost Girl!” one of them cheered as I swam.

I had always been a strong swimmer; I had a new appreciation for all the extra hours I had spent in the springs under the Hallowed Mountain.

It was only a moment later until I was nearly on top of the area where the flute player had gone under the water.

“Please, Ceru, help me,” I huffed, before taking a deep, deep breath, and then dived down underneath the water’s surface.

Carefully, I opened my eyes as I felt the pressure around my ears increase. In the bluish glow of the underwater world, I could see a glimmer of silver near the bottom of the harbor.

The rope around my waist tightened dangerously as I swam down to reach him, and my hopes sank ever so slightly; the ropes used to help pull in larger ships like the Arian one were usually long.

What if it's not enough?

I tried not to worry about it as I made my way further down. If I tugged on it now, Davar and Philia would pull me back up and I would definitely lose my chance to save the fallen soldier.

With no other alternative, I pushed forward. Thankfully, the rope loosened some a moment later.

He was still struggling a little as I caught up with him; carefully, I wrapped myself around him, linking my legs around one of his and wrapping my arms around his chest. He fought me some, but I put my hands on his face gently, before pressing my forehead to his. The chill of his helm pressed into my hair, and he seemed to realize I was trying to save him and he weakly grabbed me back.

At that, I tugged down hard on the rope and tried to swim upward. The weight of the man's armor and the increasing limpness of his body made it difficult.

For a fearful second, I wondered if we were both going to die.

But then I looked up, only to see the small circle of light above us grow larger with each small jerk of the rope.

Ceru is protecting us. It'll be alright. I know we can trust him.

Despite the desperation to breathe fresh air I felt pulsating through me, I knew we would live.

As if to pass on my reassurance, I tightened my grip on the man and pushed harder against the tides around us.

We broke through to the surface a second later, and I gulped in the fresh air, nearly laughing at the sudden burst of relief I felt.

From where we were, I could see Davar and Philia had been joined by others on the dock, and together, they were working to pull us back over to safety. I relaxed a little, focusing on the man I'd saved instead of worrying about swimming.

He coughed and sputtered, and then his eyes blinked open. He glanced around wildly before he calmed down and looked at me.

Our eyes met, and an eternal moment took hold of me. I could just see the greenish gray of his irises, clouded by fear and relief. He seemed very close to me in age; he had a straight, forthright nose and a sturdy chin. There was a bluish tint to his face, no doubt from nearly drowning and the chill of deeper waters, but he shared the porcelain complexion of his Arian kin. His hair was dark and matted to his head from the water, but I could see it was just a little darker than my own blond hair. Perhaps it was brown, or even red?

He blinked, and I finally turned away, embarrassed that I'd been staring at him; I hadn't meant to, but he was very handsome.

I'd never seen anyone as handsome as he was.

He coughed again, spitting up some more water out of his mouth.

"I've got you," I said, tightening my hold on him. The coolness of his armor pressed against my forearms and legs, and I felt a rush of excitement as he stared back at me. "You'll be all right."

"Who're you?" he asked, his voice both lyrical and gruff as he tried to compose himself.

"I'm Thessa—"

"Where is my flute?"

"I … guess you dropped it when you fell," I sputtered, suddenly feeling awkward. "I'm sorry. I don't see it."

"Great." He sighed. "Father is going to kill me."

"I'm sure he'll be happy you're alive, even if you lost your instrument," I said, trying to comfort him.

He shrugged. "Oh, well. I was wanting a new one anyway."

Before I could find anything to say to that, he smiled up at me, and I was startlingly transfixed; there was a little dimple just above the right side of his mouth, and the fullness of his lips hinted at a charming, arrogant playfulness.

"So … Thessa, was it?" he asked. "That's a pretty name."

"Thank you." My words stumbled out again as I fought against my shyness. I was glad Davar and Philia had almost finished pulling us over to the deck.

"It seems I should be the one thanking you—"

"Garrison!" An older man's voice called out from further down the dock we were approaching, despite the many sounds ringing throughout the harbor—sounds which I was proud to notice included cheers for me and praises for Ceru's providence—and I saw the man I was holding grimace.

"Great," he grumbled again. "Father's not happy at all."

I tried to glance over the dock, but I was still largely submerged in the water, and it was difficult to move without forcing the man I was holding—whose name was Garrison, it seemed—under the water once more. But with a little maneuvering, I could make out a commanding figure waiting for us at the dock, one who was ornately dressed.

"That's your father?" I asked.

"Garrison, there you are!"

Once more, Garrison jerked at the sound of his name shouted angrily. He looked over to me and put a finger to his lips as he gave me a wink. "Shhh … "

"What is it?" I asked, before his eyes closed and he went limp in my arms.

"No," I gasped, suddenly terrified he needed more medical help. What if he had an injury I couldn't see? Was it possible he'd hit his head when he'd sunk under the water?

I tried to shake him awake with no avail. I whirled around toward my friends. "Davar! Philia! Hurry and pull us in. He's fainted!"

"Garrison!" The older man's voice I'd heard before had transformed from one of anger to genuine concern, and as Davar and some of the other men laid Garrison onto the dock, I saw him kneel down before his son with anguish in his eyes.

"Wow, you were amazing, Thessa," Philia said, as she handed me my robe. She had to nudge me a few times to put it on as I watched Garrison. "That was so brave of you."

"I don't know if I actually saved him, though," I said, still only watching Garrison as his father took hold of his son's hand.

"Well, if there's anyone who can help him, it's you," Philia said with a grin. "You're a talented healer."

Davar came up to stand beside us; he seemed more comfortable now that I was back in my outer robe again. "You were reckless, Thessa. You shouldn't do things like that."

"It was nothing," I said, looking down at the ground in humble silence.

"Please." Davar scoffed. "You almost died. That's *something.* How would Phil and the rest of us go on without you?"

"Oh, Davar, stop being such a shadow caster," Philia said. "She didn't die, and neither did that young man."

"So far as we know," I murmured, turning my attention back to Garrison. He was still limply laying on the wooden dock, but there were more men coming to retrieve his body.

"Take him back to the ship," his father ordered. "Prepare my chambers and allow him to rest. And then call for the doctor. It's a good thing I decided to bring Dr. Kavia along after all."

"Wait," I called, stepping out and standing in front of Garrison's father.

The crowd had grown in the last several moments, and realizing everyone was now watching me made me falter briefly. But as Garrison's body was lifted up by six men and held in a way that reminded me too much of how we carried our dead, I forced myself to face his father and compose myself.

What am I doing? I am a Ghost ... and he is clearly someone of great importance.

Garrison's father was a strong, stern-looking man; he did not seem to be the kind of man who would worry about a child such as me under normal circumstances, but as I stood there, silent and waiting before him, I could see he was also a loving father who was wearied by the fate of his child. And I could use that, as a point of comfort.

"You're the one who saved my son," Garrison's father said. "What is it? Do you want some kind of reward?"

"Oh, no, sir. Not at all." I almost ducked my head, before I straightened my shoulders. "I am Thessa. I work as a healer in the Cathedral City medic station. I was going to say you are welcome to take him there, and I would be happy to take care of him."

He studied me with a thoughtful look on his face. "You are worried for him, then?"

"Of course," I assured him. "I might have saved him, but he clearly needs care, and quickly. And the Laenite Tribe is home to the best medics in the world, thanks to Ceru, our Dragon Guardian."

Garrison's father nodded slowly. "I see," he said. "It is true that the Laenites are well-versed in healing practices. And since you are a healer, in addition to the one who saved him, I have no choice but to take your advice in this matter."

He turned back to his men. "This lady will lead you. Take him where she says and follow her orders."

I beamed with pleasure. "Thank you, sir," I said, giving him a quick bow.

He reached out his hand, offering it to me in what I realized was a handshake. "It is lovely to meet you, Thessa," he said. The weariness of his gaze had melted away, and he looked at me with the same kind of charm that his son exuded. "I do believe I am indebted to you for saving my eldest son's life."

I almost blurted out that it was nothing again, but he took hold of my hand himself and squeezed it. "I am Ambassador Grollo Rico, of the Arian Kingdom."

The ambassador.

I felt my hand go limp in his as he shook it firmly, and I could only nod in reply. He pulled away and then gestured for me to lead the way to the medic station. It was only a few blocks, and I knew we had to get Garrison there as quickly as possible, but for some reason, the journey had never seemed to take quite so much time before.

As I worried over Garrison's health, Philia came up from behind me and grabbed my arm. "Oh, Thessa, this is wonderful, don't you think?"

"What do you mean?" I whispered back, trying not to draw attention to myself as we walked quickly through the city streets. I didn't want Grollo to start wondering if he'd made the right choice or not, and Philia's careless, cheery demeanor might have given him cause to doubt me. "A man's life is at risk."

"A young, handsome man's life is at risk," Philia corrected me with a teasing smile in her eyes. "And that is your concern most of all now, isn't it, since he owes you a Life Debt?"

"What?" I stumbled briefly, before hurriedly fighting to correct my balance.

"You saved his life. So he owes you a Life Debt," Philia reminded me. "That's the way of the Laenites, remember?"

"But he's not a Laenite," I reminded her.

"That's not how it works. A Life Debt is a Life Debt, and it's one that should be repaid." Philia giggled under her breath. "You're too noble at times, Thessa. Look how handsome he is. You can't really object to him being forced to follow you around while he's here, can you? And don't forget, Ceru's told us that those who fail to pay their debts will be punished. You wouldn't want him to get even more hurt, would you?"

"I can release him," I said. "That's always an option."

"Well, don't do it yet," Davar said as he came up from behind me. "You'll need his help if he's ever going to get his family to leave Laena."

"What do you mean?" Philia frowned.

"I talked to a few of the men," Davar whispered back to us. "The Arians are here to make an alliance."

"An alliance?" I frowned. "Why? For what?"

"For war, of course," Davar said. "The Katorians have attacked one of the Arian islands."

"What?" Philia and I both gasped.

"Fuergo's anger caused a volcanic eruption and destroyed one of the Arian islands. It's gone now, along with hundreds of people."

"Fuergo destroyed a whole island?" Philia frowned. "But I haven't heard any of those rumors."

"Just because we don't hear about them doesn't mean they don't happen, Phil."

"Don't call me 'Phil.'" She stuck her tongue out at him. "But I still think we would feel some of the damage. Or at least hear something from other traders."

"We are far enough north that we don't feel eruptions or quakes, and it might take some time to hear rumors, depending on different things." Davar ignored Philia's taunting. "The Air Dragon Guardian is upset and the king wants war with Fuergo's people."

"I know the Katorian Republic has issues with its borders," I said. "But don't you think it's possible the Arians are here for other reasons, too?"

"That's a dangerously naïve thing to say, Thessa."

"Well, it's possible, isn't it?" I clenched my fist at the side of my robes.

"Well, if Grollo Rico's here, we know it's serious." Davar glanced back at the ambassador nervously. "He's King Cressando's personal ambassador, and his son—the one you saved—is one of the king's personal minstrels and a well-known court troubadour. We'll need you to leverage the Life Debt to get them out of here before they drag us into war."

"I doubt that would happen," I said. "Father Ephyras and the other priests are the ones who oversee our country's laws. They don't want war. And neither does Ceru. We are a peaceful people, and the world knows it."

"Edmun and I train as soldiers for good reason."

I scowled at him. "Yes, for defense."

Davar sighed, and Philia rolled her eyes at him.

"Don't listen to him, Thessa," she said. "He needs to stop worrying so much."

"Or at least worry about the right things," I said, looking back at Garrison's body.

Garrison was still being carried respectfully by the men, but I thought I saw his foot push into the side of a man's head. I frowned, but the man just adjusted his hold on Garrison's leg.

I glanced over at Garrison's face; the little I could see made it seem as though he was smiling, and I hoped and prayed he would be well again soon.

"Thessa, what are you doing here?" Mother Nia's voice cut through my daydreams as she came out to meet our party.

"I'll explain as we get our newest patient settled," I said, trying to sound confident as the Arian soldiers moved to place Garrison on an empty cot. "If you can watch them for a moment, Mother Nia, I will suit up once more."

Mother Nia gazed at the soldiers with some reservation, but she quickly nodded as she saw Garrison's limp, prone figure.

"All right." She gave the men some directions, and after they were far enough away from us, she shook her head at me. "You'll have to be the one to explain this to Father Ephyras, Thessa."

"I will," I promised. "I'm certain His Eminence would have no objection to treating a man who needs care. Ceru has always given us a generous portion, and we are right to extend it to others."

It was hard not to feel a little squeamish as I waited for her approval. I didn't actually know what Ceru would think about the situation, but in a million years I could not see him disagreeing with me. As I waited for Mother Nia's response, I couldn't help but hope I would gain more clarity at her words. I had grown up with Ceru and the teachings of the Cathedral, and I had learned my lessons in language and persuasion well. I didn't know if I was right, but I knew enough that it sounded right, and that was good enough for now.

"Of course," Mother Nia finally agreed. There was still a sense of irritation in her voice. "But Father Ephyras might not necessarily see it that way."

She was not wrong; Father Ephyras often disagreed with me, and I would have to prepare myself for any possible punishment. But I was a little disappointed.

Still, I knew I couldn't hesitate. I muttered out a quick excuse, and then went to make Garrison as comfortable as possible.

CHAPTER THREE

※ ※ ※ ※

Roughly an hour passed before Grollo was finally convinced to leave his son's side.

Garrison was still unconscious, but it was getting late, and having several Arian soldiers in the medical station unnerved some of the other healers.

"It was a great honor to meet you, Thessa." Grollo reached out his hand for mine in another handshake. "I am vastly relieved to know my son is in excellent care, and by such a thoughtful and talented young lady as yourself."

"Thank you," I said. "I can speak for the talented medics around here, and I can assure you once we know what is wrong with him, we will contact you."

"Thank you."

Grollo was clearly a good man who was only worried about his son, but it was still nice when he and his men left.

Once the Arians were gone, the other medics relaxed, and I was just happy I could take care of Garrison myself without an audience.

That also meant I could look at him some more without feeling embarrassed. I hid a smile I as pulled a chair up beside Garrison, eager to watch over him.

But just as I sat down, his eyes opened up.

"You're awake," I gasped, stunned. "Oh, this is so good to—"

"Did they leave?" he asked, and I just stood there for a long moment, before I understood what had happened.

Strange disappointment sank through me. I leaned back in my chair, slumping over a little. "You've been awake this entire time, haven't you?"

Garrison grinned mischievously. "Well, after I lost my flute, I had a feeling my father wouldn't be too happy with me. I know he seems like a nice guy to you, and I'm sure he can be, but in truth he has a wicked temper, especially when it comes to me. I figured if I'd fainted, I'd get less of a diatribe when I get back to our ship."

My stomach twisted into another knot. I felt betrayed. "You lied."

Garrison saw my face and shrugged. “Please, Thessa, you mean to tell me that *you've* never lied about something?”

“All Ceru's children strive to tell the truth,” I said, which only made him laugh.

“So that's a yes, huh?” He scooted over in his bed and motioned for me to come and sit next to him on the cot. “Why don't you come up here and keep me company for a little while? I'd hate to think I've upset you now.”

I frowned at him, but he only smiled more brightly.

“Please, Thessa. Give me a chance to make it up to you. I'd like to get to know the woman who saved my life. No reason we can't steal a little time from life's demands, right?”

“Well … ” I glanced out a nearby window, looking at the Cathedral's shadow in the background. In all the excitement, I'd forgotten that today was my Adoption Day, and I was supposed to meet with Father Ephyras tonight. By that point, I was sure it was too late to go and see him. He would have to come and find me.

Once he hears about Garrison, I am sure he will understand why I didn't show up.

I bit back a sigh. I could understand why Garrison was so quick to lie; his father might be cruel, but at least it was his father. The High Priest who oversaw the whole Laenite Tribe would likely not be happy with me, especially from what Mother Nia had said earlier.

And if Father Ephyras hears that Garrison was faking his injury, he'll be even more upset.

"Well, I suppose I can stay for a little longer," I finally said. "And I suppose I should check you over for any real concerns. But I am good with sitting here, thank you."

Garrison gave me a cheeky wink. "Aren't you so innocent and sweet?"

"You might want to keep your voice down. If any of the other medics see or hear you, they'll send word to your father," I said.

"Oh, thanks for letting me know." He gave me another teasing smirk. "If someone else comes in, I'll be sure to faint again and prolong my visit here."

I couldn't stop myself from grinning. "You know, most of my patients are more eager to leave the hospital than they are to stay."

"If you are their nurse, I can't imagine why."

I felt a small, red flush come over my cheeks, but Garrison didn't make me feel embarrassed, exactly; he made me feel like someone was seeing me, the real me, for the first time. Many Ghost Children grew up with a stigma surrounding them, and so it was just nice to sit there and chat with someone who didn't see us as merely workers.

And Garrison was quite funny and engaging. For the next hour, he told me stories about King Cressando and the different Arian islands, including how he was a musician, even though his father really wanted him to follow in his footsteps as a future ambassador.

I envied him a little at first, and then a lot more as he continued. Garrison had seen so much more of the world than I had. Garrison told me stories of the king's court, as well as several stories of his tricks and antics aboard his father's ship, and the various times he'd been allowed to accompany his father on his trips. He told me about how he'd impersonated a messenger from Yla, and organized a play about Atlaris based on a legend he'd made up.

My favorite story was how he'd sneaked away from his father's palace on Kestra, one of the smaller islands, and he'd been able to visit the Floating Gardens, one of their national treasures and a frequent tourist attraction open to travelers from all over the world.

"Even the Katorians?" I asked.

Garrison's eyes suddenly darkened into a deadly storm, and I swallowed hard. Clearly, I'd made a mistake in mentioning them. Seeing nothing else to do, I tried to smooth over my mistake.

"I've heard the rumors that your nation is going to war with them, but that's not true, is it?" I asked. "I mean, your country is beautiful, and your people are dedicated to music and art and beauty. War doesn't seem like something you would do."

"Ugliness naturally seeks to conquer and consume beauty," Garrison said. "The Katorians are no longer welcome on our shores. They have been our trade partners for many years, but now, they are using their Fire Dragon to sink our islands, and we must stop them. People are dying, Thessa."

He took my hand. "You wouldn't want that for your people, would you?"

“Of course not.” I tightened my hand around his. “I am sorry for your loss. I hope those who have died are safe in the Eternal Hall of the Creator.”

“Well, they are safer in death, perhaps, but that doesn’t mean much for the rest of us,” Garrison said. His eyes further darkened, this time with grief. “My mother was one of the ones we lost.”

“Oh, that’s awful.” I pressed both of my hands into his and pulled it up to my cheek. My own heart stirred with pain as my eyes stung with unshed tears.

“It’s been a few months,” Garrison said stoically. “It was during one of Fuergo’s temper tantrums. Mother had a private mansion on one of the smaller islands. Her island had a volcano on it, and it erupted. The lava consumed everything.”

Garrison didn’t have to tell me anything further. I could picture it inside my mind. A beautiful woman was sitting in a spectacular house, peacefully going about her day, and in the next moment, she was incinerated along with everything else.

“I’m so sorry,” I said again, having nothing else to say.

"Well, I only wish the Katorians were," Garrison sneered. "They've refused any responsibility and they refuse to pay us any damages. As if they could do anything that would make up for Mother's death. But now, they've attacked us."

"That's terrible," I said. "Where?"

"They attacked us in Triumphia. It's in Kator, but it's always been a safe port for Arian ships and traders. Until now. It's no longer safe for any foreigner."

I frowned. "Triumphia? That's not too far away from here."

"Which is part of the reason we have come," Garrison said. "We're here to warn you that Laena might be next, if they are not stopped. It's clear now that they want to take our land and enslave us. They have no regard for human life or its beauty or value. They've had issues with the Earth Dragon Guardian for years, and now they hate us, too."

"I don't know what to say to that," I whispered, horrified. "This is just so—"

"Thessa? What are you still doing here?"

Of all the voices in the world, Kana's was the last possible one I wanted to hear while I was talking with Garrison. She stepped into the room and Garrison fell back against his pillow in another fake faint.

"Kana." I stood up and tried to conceal the sourness I felt in my soul at her sudden arrival. "What is it?"

"Father Siah sent a note to the station," she said, holding up a folded piece of paper. "You're supposed to report to the Hallowed Mountain as soon as you're able. He was concerned when you didn't return for your meeting earlier."

"Oh." I had a feeling from the way she said it that she had held onto the note for some time.

"You had better get going." Kana's eyes narrowed with wicked pleasure. "But don't worry. I'm sure I can take over caring for your patient while you attend to your other duties. Besides, he might want to try some of his stories out on a new audience. You've been talking for over an hour."

"We have?" I didn't feel like I contributed a whole lot to the conversation, but Garrison's voice had been so comforting and entertaining.

As if he took that to be an invitation, Garrison's eye opened up. "I'm always up for charming an audience."

"I'm sure you are," Kana agreed with a smile. "But are you sure you don't want to actually rest? It's almost midnight."

I looked out the window again, only to see the moon was high in the sky. I took comfort in knowing Kana's shift would be over soon, even though I didn't want her to spend any time with Garrison at all.

"I suppose I better leave," I said. I brightened as an idea struck me. "Kana, you can take over for now. And you'll need to start by heading over to the Arian ship in the harbor and letting his father, Ambassador Rico, know that he's woken up."

There was no need to tell the ambassador Garrison had been up for a few hours.

Garrison met my eyes with his. "I always love an audience," he assured me. "But I like having friends, too."

Kana laughed as she handed me the note and started fluffing Garrison's pillows. "She's more like your creditor, I'm afraid. Or hasn't she told you about the Life Debt you owe her now, since she saved you?"

"Life Debt?" Garrison looked confused.

"There's no need to worry about that now," I said hesitantly. If Garrison was telling me the truth about the Katorians and the Fire Dragon Republic, Davar might have had a good point earlier. Laena did not want to go to war, and we also didn't want to give the Katorians a reason to push us into one.

I decided I would have to ask Father Ephyras about the situation. He was the one who was in charge of our tribe, after all. He would be the one who would know what to do with Garrison's information.

And while I was meeting with him, I recalled, I would get to hear the news of my future. I had been called to the Hallowed Mountain, and Ceru would be there, with news for me.

As Kana finished taking Garrison's pulse, I gripped the note in my hand. "I'll be back tomorrow, Garrison. In the meantime, Kana here will take care of you, and you should rest."

"Thank you, Thessa." Garrison gave me one of his charming smiles, enough to where I could see the shadow of his dimple just above the left corner of his lips. It was joyful torture to look at his face, and it only made me more sad to leave him.

I smiled. "I'll look forward to our next visit."

Even with Kana there, I couldn't help but feel excited as I left. Garrison made my heart swell and ache at the same time, and I didn't have to wonder if I could fall in love with him.

CHAPTER FOUR

※ ※ ※ ※

As I entered the Hallowed Mountain, I felt the familiar tug of belonging at the back of my heart. While I knew it was far from the family I longed for, this place was the closest thing I had ever known to a home. The goodness I had experienced here gave me the hope my joy would be even greater when I had a family of my own.

My clothes were dry from rescuing Garrison, but I still slipped into my quarters and put on a fresh outfit. I was already late, so a few moments to look less rumpled and my face a little less weary wouldn't cost me much more than I'd already lost. It might even give me a few more points, looking as special as I did, I thought, putting on my lacy habit.

The lace trimmings of my frock complimented my white, fur-lined boots, and added a touch of frivolity and fun to my look.

Father Ephyras would likely see it as a way to call attention to myself, an act of arrogance or self-importance.

"But Ceru will like it," I murmured to myself, thinking of him with a smile.

The Great Sea Serpent was the ruler of my tribe, but he was also my friend, and if I had to choose between pleasing Ceru and Father Ephyras, I always chose Ceru.

I whisked my way along the hidden halls of the Cathedral. Behind the public sanctuary and classrooms, built into the mountain were quarters where the High Priests slept. This is also where the other Ghost Children resided until we were released from our Life Debts and given a new role in our community.

I loved living in a place that held secrets within secrets; it made me feel more at home.

Especially knowing that I had secrets of my own—although my nighttime visits to Ceru hardly seemed like secrets.

From the wanderings I would take when I was younger, unable to sleep at night, I knew there was another secret staircase in the adjoining hallway, one that would lead me down into the heart of Ceru's nest.

But this time, I kept moving forward, past that door and through another one. The note Kana had given me said Father Siah and Father Ephyras were waiting for me on the balcony across from Ceru's nest, where the priests often held their meetings with Ceru and each other.

I walked down the long hall, feeling the slow incline down into the bottom of the mountain. Even if I didn't see it, or its end, I felt my body chill and my breath turned white.

After a few moments, I finally entered into the mountain's atrium. The water was clear at the top and murky at the bottom, giving the illusion that it was an upside-down sky; little streams trickled down the walls, endlessly cycling through the stages of water, fog, and dew. There were even swabs of luminescent algae lighting up the cave and the indoor spring under the mountain, their light bouncing playfully off Ceru's shining scales as the Great Sea Serpent slept across the water from the balcony's edge.

I could see Father Ephyras talking with Father Siah near the balcony's railing. I stayed still for a long moment, wanting to take everything in and remember this moment clearly for the rest of my life.

After all, this was the last moment of my ordinary life, wasn't it? Knowing that added a layer of anticipation and appreciation to the inside of the mountain's spring.

"Thessa. There you are."

I turned to see Father Siah approaching me.

"Father Siah," I said respectfully, giving him a warm smile and quick bow. "I apologize for my lateness."

"I'm sure," he replied, his voice dry enough he knew I wasn't really that sorry. Still, he didn't question me on it, and I had a feeling he had been informed of my movements.

"I will ask for your forgiveness," I added quickly.

"You already have it." As if we were both thinking the same thing, we looked over at Father Ephyras standing by the balcony's railing. "From me, anyway."

Father Siah had been a priest here for several years, and over the course of those years, we had always been close. I knew him well enough I could often read his mind, even if we both knew we weren't allowed to say what it was that passed between us.

"Are you ready?" Father Siah asked, holding out his arm. "Today is a day you will never forget, Thessa."

I hesitated. "I think so," I murmured honestly. "I've waited for this for a long time."

"You don't even know what it is," Father Siah reminded me. There was a small smile on his face, one that seemed like he was sad, or that he was possibly teasing me. "Come and see."

I nodded and took his arm. "You're right. Thanks."

He patted my hand with a surprising amount of affection. "You look so much like your mother."

"I do?" I was caught off guard by Father Siah's admission. As a priest, Father Siah was honor-bound to keep the secrets of the High Priests, and that included information regarding the Ghost Children. Many of us who had been adopted at birth longed to know the truth about our heritage, but we also knew that our blood did not define us—even if we still wondered about it. But Father Siah did not have a repentant look on his face as we approached the High Priest, even if he refused to look me in the eye.

"Forgive me," he said, clearing his throat. "I misspoke."

His apology was as insincere as mine had been, and if Father Ephyras hadn't been there, I might have said something. But before I could demand a better explanation, Father Ephyras greeted me.

"Thessa, how good of you to come," he said. His voice was grave and low, but there was enough of an echo around us that I could hear the supposedly-hidden irritation.

I bowed my head. "I apologize for my delay. I assure you it was not intentional."

"I have been informed of your activities, and I must thank you for saving that young man's life. I trust you are well, yourself?" Father Ephyras looked me over carefully. "It is not yet that warm. I trust the harbor won't cause you to turn ill?"

"No sign of anything so far," I said. I glanced over at Ceru, who had his long, scaly body curled up into a bored-looking flop, and if we had been alone, I might've laughed at his own irreverence. "I am used to the water."

"Yes. I know." Father Ephyras scowled. He was an old man, and a bitter one, too, which added to his age and demeanor more than the wrinkles of his brow ever could. He cleared his throat and straightened the little box-like hat on his head. That was when I noticed he was wearing his most formal set of ceremonial robes, the long white ones that called for special occasions. As nice as it was that it was my Adoption Day, I couldn't remember him ever doing that before.

"Well, happy Adoption Day to you, Thessa, a Ghost Child of Ceru, a daughter of the Laenite Tribe and a protected and treasured heir of the Great Sea Serpent," Father Ephyras intoned, bringing on the usual formalities.

He listed off some more titles and some history, but I noticed that his eyes slid back to Ceru each time he took a breath, as though he was waiting for something.

When he finally finished, I nodded and bowed again, to show my acceptance. "Thank you, Father."

"On this day, the fifteenth anniversary of your adoption into Ceru's abode, we celebrate by giving you a special gift."

It was traditional for small gifts to be given out on Adoption Day. Last year I had received a handwoven bookmark designed by Mother Nia herself, since I was going to become a medic like her. And as much as I treasured it, all I really wanted was a family.

My fingers tightened around the skirt of my long robes.

This is it, right? I'll finally know who it is I'll marry. Who it is I'll start a family with.

"Ceru himself would like to speak with you in private," Father Ephyras murmured, before he moved out of the way and allowed me to see Ceru directly.

Momentarily, I faltered. I had always sneaked away to see Ceru, but it was not traditional for Ceru to talk to anyone but the priests, especially in cases like this, where it was a matter of ceremony and tradition.

Perhaps because we were such good friends, Ceru didn't feel the need to talk to me through the priests? I looked over at Father Siah, whose hands were folded tightly in strained prayer as his gaze was fixed firmly on the rocky floor.

As I glanced back at Ceru, he finally woke up from his slumber. He untwisted his long, ancient body, reaching his long neck toward the balcony. I could hear the slimy flicker of the scales as they moved, almost like a waterfall moving each droplet of water at a time.

Ceru was called the Great Sea Serpent for good reason; he was almost like a large snake, with flared fins at his joints and on his tail. He had gills that opened and closed with his breathing, and when I would fall asleep next to him at night, I would swear I could hear his heart gently thundering. He was a monster of a dragon.

But I never feared him. His eyes were large dark orbs, full of moving mist and mystic secrets. The first time I'd seen him, he'd stared at me for a long time, before I heard my name coming from him.

"Thessa."

He called to me now, the same as he always had, and I smiled. I reached out to him as he approached me, opening my arms so I could put a hand on each of his cheeks.

It was a habit I'd done countless times before, but even as I realized it wasn't likely what Father Ephyras or Father Siah wanted me to do, Ceru was already giving me his dragon-like smile and sinking between my open arms.

His head was more broad than my body, but it was our version of a hug, and after all the excitement of my day, I wanted to share what happened—and how I was worried about possible war—with my closest friend.

"Sorry I was late," I whispered as I held him. "It's a long story."

"One I am sure I will listen to later," Ceru whispered back. *"Right now, I have been given a word for you, and it is my hope you will take it."*

"Of course." A small giggle escaped me. "I've been waiting to hear what you'll say to me for fifteen years now."

"Well, then, let me not keep you waiting any longer, my beloved Thessa." Ceru pressed himself further into me, and I could feel his gentle power.

"You don't need to cry for me," I said, recognizing his movement. "No one is hurt right now that needs one of your dragon tears, Ceru."

As the Water Dragon Guardian, Ceru's tears had the power to help heal deep wounds; they were powerful enough to bring people back from death, if they were administered in time. I'd asked Ceru about it once, and he said that each tear was a pain he was willing to take away and keep for himself. He would give the tear to someone, and then he would take it upon himself.

He seemed to know I was thinking this as he nudged me with his nose. *"I didn't choose you to be able to catch my tears, Thessa. Do you know why you are able to retrieve them for me?"*

"You didn't choose me?" I almost felt a little betrayed at his admission; I had been able to collect tears from Ceru since I'd become a medic and first told Ceru of a patient I wasn't sure would make it.

"When you were a little girl, you came down here looking for a place to hide—a place to cry in private," Ceru told me. His eyes were flooding with light and power now, and I held steady, prepared to catch his tears. *"I gave you a place to do just that, and over the years, you have poured your heart and love out to me as you cried."*

"So … you're giving me a tear?" I asked, uncertain of what he was saying.

"No. I am giving you a blessing far greater," he said. *"As you know, the world is changing, and unrest is brewing. The Age of Dragons is coming to an end."*

"What do you mean?" I asked, pulling back, ever so slightly. "Ceru, this is hardly the gift I wanted. I was hoping you would tell me who I would marry."

Ceru's nostrils twitched in tired amusement. *"I haven't forgotten. But right now, I am telling you that the world is changing, and we will change with it. I need someone like you to be there, in the heart of this trouble, to remind others who we are and our place in this world. You are a woman who knows the power found in sorrow and the gifts that can be found only in tears."*

As Ceru finished speaking to me, the tears finally flourished from out of his eyes. The large, light-filled droplets trailed down either side of his face, trickling down from the long, narrow slits to the softness of under his chin, until they came together.

Without hesitation, I held out my hands as it dropped.

The water didn't slosh into my palms, as I expected; instead, it slid down and gently nestled itself on my hands. I gazed at it in shock and surprise and honor, and also confusion and uncertainty and wonder.

And then another bright light appeared, blinding me. I didn't let go of it, but I did look away. But when I looked back, the tear of light and Ceru's power had formed into an amulet. It wasn't any bigger than the size of my hand, but I saw it was a golden dragon, with a large sapphire-colored gem in the middle.

"This … is for me?" I asked, awed as much as I was uncertain.

"Yes, Thessa." Ceru nodded, and then pressed his nose to my forehead affectionately. *"You are to be my Handmaiden, the mother of the new age, and the one who will bear a child who will wield all the powers of the dragons."*

"I'll be a mother." A shiver of excitement ran through me. "What about my family?" I asked. "Can't you tell me anything about the man I'll marry?"

His great dragon eyes rolled, clearly exasperated by my persistence. *"Thessa."*

"Please?" I begged. "Please, Ceru. Give me something. Please?"

Finally, Ceru nodded wearily. *"You will marry a man who comes from outside the Laenite Tribe. He will be a man who looks at you and sees your true value, even when you do not see it yourself. He will love you unconditionally, even unto death."*

"And I am sure I'll love him, too," I whispered happily. "What is his name?"

"That is all I will tell you for now. We will speak again of the future after your Life Debt is fulfilled."

And then he slivered away, heading back to his nest. I watched as he curled up again, seeming to fall back asleep.

For a moment, I paused, watching him. I had never seen him so slow and sloppy in his movements.

I held onto the amulet; I still had no specific details about the man I would marry or how I would meet him. But Ceru had said much about the world; surely, he knew what was happening even now.

Surely, Ceru even knew about Garrison. I blushed at the thought.

Father Ephyras cleared his throat behind me. "Well, Thessa? What did Ceru tell you?"

I was grateful that Ceru had kept our conversation private, even if it was not all I wanted to hear. I held up the amulet as I told Father Ephyras what Ceru had told me, that I would marry someone from outside the Laenite Tribe. Father Siah's eyes swelled up with tears as I allowed him to examine the Ceru's gift to me.

"This is the Crest of Ceru, the one which marks Ceru's chosen Handmaiden," Father Siah said, his voice full of awe. "You are to be the mother of the new age."

"Ceru told me so," I assured him, remembering my other reason for joy. I would have my own child. My eyes glazed over in happy daydreams at the thought of a son or daughter in my arms, just like the little ones from the medic station. I barely realized Father Ephyras was clearly upset.

"How could he choose *her*?" He threw up his hands, and then shook his head. "This is outrageous."

"It is the will of our Lord the Creator," Father Siah said, his voice still soft, but much more angry. "Father, calm yourself."

Father Ephyras scoffed, and for a moment, I swore I saw a gleam of animosity in Father Ephyras' gaze; I stepped back, worried he would lunge at me or strike Father Siah.

After a few long, steadying breaths, he steadied himself. "This is … well, you can see this is a very important occasion. Some might even wonder if this was the right call?"

He lifted his head toward Ceru, just as Ceru's tail whipped through the water in an icy reply. The small slice of water splashed Father Ephyras from head to toe.

"Oh, my." As I did my best to swallow my laughter, watching Father Ephyras wipe off the spray in disgust, Father Siah handed me back the Crest.

"This is a huge honor, Thessa. You are now the chosen Handmaiden, and you carry all the Laenite hopes and legacy with you." He looked down at me with paternal pride. "I knew you were special."

I was surprised to see a tear flowing down Father Siah's cheek, and I was even more surprised as the amulet lit up, its ambience bouncing off Father Siah's tear.

"That's enough. It's late, and you've had a very long day. Not to mention we have more duties for you to attend to in the morning," Father Ephyras said behind me. "If you are going to be Ceru's Handmaiden, you will need to prepare yourself. There are rituals for this. Education, purification, and study … there is so much to do. Go to bed, Thessa."

I nodded slowly, still trying to process everything that happened and all the questions I longed to ask. Seeing my vacillation, Father Siah took my arm again and led me to the stairwell.

Before I left, I suddenly remembered what Davar and Garrison had said about war. "Father Ephyras," I called. "I wanted to ask you about the Katorians. I've been told the Arians were attacked at Triumphia. Do you think the Katorian Republic is heading toward war?"

"From the little the ambassador and I have spoken of, I know enough that they have been preparing for it for some time," Father Ephyras said. "But it is not something I wish to discuss with you, Thessa. You might be the Handmaiden to Ceru, but this is a matter of politics and war. I would rather leave you out of it."

"I don't know if I'm granted the right to speak on it, but I wish to be included," I said, trying to keep the hardness out of my voice. I had friends that would be in danger, and Garrison had lost his mother from Fuergo's raging. If I was to carry the future and legacy of the Laenite people, I wanted to see to its care.

Perhaps it was because I felt frustrated at Ceru's reluctance to tell me the name of the man I would marry, but I wanted to make sure I honored the duties I was specifically given—especially since it looked like I would be met with opposition, given the look on Father Ephyras' face.

Ceru has just gifted me with this honor, and already Father Ephyras is trying to discard me.

Father Ephyras looked livid at my remark. As he struggled to respond, Father Siah pulled at my sleeve.

"Right now is not a good time, Thessa," he said. "It has been a long day of work for you, and there will be time in the future to discuss these things. Right now, you are better off getting some sleep. You've been given a great honor. We need not worry about war right now. If anything, we should celebrate."

"Celebrate? Celebrate what?" I asked.

"Being the Handmaiden to Ceru is no small honor," Father Siah said. "And Ambassador Grollo mentioned he would like to hold a party in your honor, since you saved his son. The Spiritual Mothers are working with some of his servants to prepare a feast."

"Oh, there's no need to do that," I said, blushing before stifling a yawn. Perhaps

Father Siah was right about the rest, I thought.

"Nonsense. It won't harm us any to allow them to help plan a banquet for you. At least, the Priests and Spiritual Mothers don't think so," Father Siah said. There was a small twitch at the side of his lips, enough to make me wonder if he didn't agree with himself, but before I could ask, he smiled warmly. "It seems you've made quite an impression on people tonight, Thessa."

As Father Siah led me back to my room, I clutched the amulet to my heart and nodded. I was honored to have been chosen, I really was; but I was also thinking back to Garrison as I gave in and allowed myself to be escorted out of Ceru's resting place.

Of all people I'd made an impression on, I hoped I'd especially made a good one on him.

CHAPTER FIVE

※ ※ ※ ※

"This is great!"

I watched as Philia piled her small plate full of Laenite desserts and I tried not to envy how happy and carefree she was as she sat down next to me. While the Laenites and the Arian visitors reveled in their haphazardly prepared party, Philia was able to indulge all of her fantasies. I was happy for her, but I knew there were several Priests and Spiritual Mothers who were watching me with scrutiny, and the thought of all that attention made me conscientious and uncomfortable.

Philia's twin sister, Pia, sat down with a groan on the other side of her. "Come on, Philia," she begged. "Everyone can see us from up here. Don't make a fuss."

Philia stuck out her tongue, which was covered in a thin layer of white icing and honey glaze from the pastry she was currently devouring. She took a drink and swallowed. "You know, sometimes I think it's more likely that you're Davar's sister, rather than mine."

"No one would claim you but me," Pia replied, as she took a dainty bite of her own crumpet. "Right, Thessa?"

"If you're worried about a scene, maybe you should use Thessa's new, proper title," Philia teased, nudging me with her arm. "Isn't that right, Handmaiden Thessa?"

When she saw I didn't care for her teasing, she sighed. "Oh, come on. Don't be such a bore. Lighten up. After all, this is technically your party."

"But I haven't even done anything yet for Laena," I said.

In truth, I felt a little guilty. The night of my fifteenth Adoption Day, Father Siah had taken me back to my room, and I had fully intended to wait a little while and then sneak back down to talk to Ceru. But it seemed as soon as I saw my bed, all my unknown tiredness caught up with me, and I fell asleep. I was not able to get up early enough to see him before the day started, and Father Ephyras, among others, had managed to keep me moving and busy for the past week while Ambassador Grollo and some of Cathedral City's elders and deaconesses scrambled around to put a party together.

As if it sensed my uncertainty, the amulet, the Crest of Ceru, bumped against my breastbone. I wore it around my neck, keeping it close to my heart but still free from others' scrutiny. I pressed against it, seeing it as a source of comfort.

At first, it had been nice to have the others express their joy for me as Ceru's Handmaiden, but as the days passed, I noticed many of them were apologetic when it came to the subject of marriage. It seemed they'd heard I wasn't going to be married just yet, and no one knew who it would be, so it was a disappointment.

And they weren't exactly wrong, either.

I clasped my hands together in my lap, trying not to feel my own pangs of loneliness and frustration. I had been hoping to come away from my meeting with Father Ephyras and Ceru with some news of who my husband would be, but no name had been spoken, and neither had an exact timeline been established.

I did have one specific detail: Ceru said I would marry someone from outside of Laena.

That was all I had—for now.

At that, I glanced around again, craning my neck around the crowds. A moment later, I just picked at my plate distastefully and sighed. “Besides, Garrison is not here.”

“Oh, so that’s the real reason you’re upset,” Philia said as she laughed.

“Stop it,” I hissed. “I don’t need you embarrassing me in addition to yourself.”

“Phil’s always looking for a chance to do just that,” Davar said as he approached. Beside him was our other friend, Edmun, who only had a surly look on his face.

“There you are, Edmun,” I said. “I saw they have fried manna down there next to the stuffed quailfish and thought of you.”

Edmun gave me a gracious nod. He was, just like the others, a little younger than me, but he was one of my friends who was better at maintaining his composure, even if he was upset. To see him this ruffled made me concerned, but he brushed my concern away.

“Some of those Arian soldiers have been causing trouble all week, that’s all,” he said. “I’ve had to escort several of them out of different upper rooms over the last week. You’ll have to forgive me if I see this party as an excuse for them to indulge in more gluttony and drunkenness.”

"I'm sure it's just because they've been traveling for several days," I said. "I imagine they're just happy to be back on land."

Edmun snorted. "Don't make their excuses for them, Thessa. It's not a good idea to imagine them one way when they're clearly not."

"Oh, come on, you two," Philia said. "Thessa's sad because one guy didn't show up, Edmun's upset he finally had to do a little more work than usual, and Davar and Pia are combining forces against me. No wonder I'm as excited and energetic as three or more people; I've got to balance all of your humors out."

I giggled and then leaned against her shoulder. "And we are all thankful for it."

The rest of my friends followed my lead and allowed Philia's exuberance to distract us. Even if I continued to look for Garrison when she wasn't looking my way, I appreciated her effervescence.

Just as I was beginning to feel hopelessly alone, the hauntingly beautiful sound of a flute drifted through Cathedral City's main courtyard.

And then I saw him.

Garrison appeared, standing in the middle of the crowd, playing his tune. Other Arian soldiers slowly stood up around him, pulling out their own instruments.

"Oh, this is amazing," Philia said as they all began to play. "They're going to perform for us after all!"

Philia was right. The music took off, echoing throughout the whole city. The Arians were known for their artistic skills, and their music was palpable, so rich and real I thought I could feel the notes in the air as they swirled around me.

It didn't take long for more to rise up and start dancing. I had to swallow a chuckle, watching the Arians forcefully pull out Laenites to get them to dance. We sang, we played, and we performed; but largely, dancing was not our favorite expression of joy, unless it was at a wedding.

I saw Father Ephyras glaring at me from another one of the head tables. From his expression, I almost thought I could read his mind as people danced between us.

This is not a wedding.

I took a drink from my cup to escape his gaze. By the time I put the cup down, I felt a little more resolved. Ceru himself said I would marry an outsider to our people, something which was nearly unheard of; it was time to start thinking about more than just the tribe and our people. We had the world to think of, too.

And in some ways, we had ignored it long enough. Laena was far enough north that even Triumphia, the northernmost city of Kator, was several days' worth of sailing and at least a week away by horse. And while the Arians were apparently struggling with them, the Katorians seemed content to let us have the colder dragonlands; perhaps they even feared Ceru's power as the Sea Serpent, since they were people of the Fire Dragon.

As I was caught up in my thoughts, Philia started to cough and Pia gasped, while Davar and Edmun both stood up. I looked up to see Garrison was grinning down at me.

"Well, Handmaiden, how about a dance?" he asked, reaching his hand out for mine.

I blushed profusely, and Pia had to pull me out of my chair.

"Of course, she would love to!" Pia said, clearly filling in for Philia as she continued to cough up powdered sugar from her latest dessert.

I didn't have time to thank Pia as Garrison tugged me through Davar and Edmun's protective frowns and twirled me into a dance.

"I don't know," I warned Garrison, finally finding my voice.

"Come on, what's not to know? I will show you how to dance, if that's what's keeping you back," Garrison said. "Just keep your balance and trust me."

Trust me.

It was such a lovely call to adventure—even if it was one I knew Father Ephyras would not want me indulging myself in.

He never seemed to want me to have any adventure at all, truth be told.

As we swooped around the room and Garrison turned me into several spins, I soon found myself breathless with laughter and joy.

"You're a good dancer," I said a few moments later, struggling to catch my breath. I tripped over his foot, but he managed to catch me and straighten my posture without a pause.

"Well, then, perhaps you'll have to add it to my slave duties," Garrison replied.

When I gave him a quizzical look, he smiled again. "I was reliably informed by some of your friends that Laenites subscribe to the old traditions, including the Life Debt."

"It is tied to honor," I replied, prepared to defend our ways against his clear amusement.

Garrison stopped me. "Oh, Thessa, it's fine. My father actually said that in agreeing to the Life Debt, this would be something we could do to strengthen our relationship with you and your people. So you may consider me your slave now."

I frowned at his mistake; the Life Debt was not an agreement between parties. How did he not know this? I softened a little; perhaps Aria was not as diligent in teaching her charges as Ceru had been with us.

But I did want to correct him. The Life Debt was more of a bond, and it wasn't really a master and slave relationship. It was more akin to adoption, a bond of family and brotherhood. But before I say anything, he continued talking.

"I'm perfectly agreeable to be under your mastery, too; the fact that you've been promoted to Handmaiden to Ceru the Great Serpent must mean you are to become a great leader. And our friendship is surely a sign of coming providence for all of us."

I tightened my hand around his. "That is true," I agreed, glad he seemed to share the same reverence toward Ceru's power as I did.

Garrison twirled me around again, before pulling me close into him. I looked into his gray-green eyes and leaned more fully into him.

"So, my lovely friend, my Handmaiden Thessa, tell me what you would have me do for you."

His voice was sweet enough it nearly made my knees buckle, and the way he said my name was just lightly seductive, making me feel weak and shameful. Enjoying myself seemed wrong, even as I couldn't stop myself from wanting more.

Behind us, I could see Ambassador Grollo and Father Siah watching us. Father Siah wore a bland look on his face, but Garrison's father was nothing but cheerful.

Further up the table, I saw Father Ephyras scowling fiercely, and at the sight, that sense of resolution cloaked me again.

The Laenites were seen around the world as people who were averse to change, but as

Ceru said, the world was changing, and we would change with it. And I could be useful in helping them do so, couldn't I?

And Garrison would be, too. He already was part of the change

So I met Garrison's gaze as boldly as I could.

"Dance with me," I said. I tightened my grip on Garrison's hands, allowing myself to trust him.

The rest of the party raged on, but for the rest of the night, Garrison stayed by my side, adding a magical quality to my night.

Even when I grew too tired to keep dancing, he performed for me, he sang for me, he played his flute for me; he even introduced me to some of his friends from the ship.

By the time the party was over, even though I could not exactly pinpoint the moment, I knew that the magical quality of the night was no coincidence; as I looked up into Garrison's eyes, there was a fullness in my heart and only twisted knots in my stomach.

I was in love.

I had not fallen into love; it was just something that happened. One moment, I was alone and waiting for my family, and then the next, I felt love capture me, like a butterfly surrounded securely in the heart of a net.

Ceru had said I would marry outside of the Laenite Tribe, and he'd said it on the very day I'd rescued Garrison.

Surely others could see it, too.

Garrison was everything I'd wanted in a husband—smart, good-looking, and strong. He was gifted with a social ease that could help solidify the Arian Kingdom with the Laenite Tribe.

And it would be a big benefit to Laena, too. The Arians were already well-known throughout the world for their artisans, merchants, and builders. With Garrison's connection to the king and his courts, it could help bring about more peace to the world.

I said nothing to Garrison about my feelings, but as he stayed beside me—all the while joking with his friends and mine about how he was "enslaved" by our new bond—I believed he felt something for me, too.

When it was time to go, Garrison took my hand and kissed it gallantly. It was the perfect way to end the night, but Garrison went a step further.

His hand reached up and cupped my cheek delicately, the sly smile on his face full of his trademark charm.

"If you approve it, Handmaiden Thessa, I vow that as long as I am here in Laena, I will come and visit you each day from now on."

"Yes." I barely felt myself nod in agreement, too busy wishing he would lean over and kiss me. "Yes, I'd love that."

Later on, as I fell asleep in my bed, I feverishly prayed Garrison and his people would stay with us for a long, long time.

CHAPTER SIX

※ ※ ※ ※

"What do you mean, they're leaving?"

It was a few days later when I stared down at Father Siah as he sat at his desk, my mouth hanging open. As if it meant absolutely nothing, he'd just informed me Garrison and the rest of the Arians would be leaving the following morning.

I recovered as swiftly as I could, but dread trickled through me. The last few days had been full of magic, each one blurring over with excitement and enchantment as I spent my time between shifts with Garrison and plenty of others in Cathedral City.

Since I'd saved Garrison's life, plenty of Arians had come to meet me and talk with me; some of them wanted my perspective on what they called "the coming war," and I was grateful when Garrison would brush their fears away and dismiss their claims.

"All will be well," he said. "But it's really too grand a day to let Thessa worry over such things, isn't it?"

Some of my own tribe members echoed their questions, and when I did speak on what I knew, it was mostly to say Father Ephyras was the one who was leading the council of Priests and Spiritual Mothers in that regard.

And that was the truth, even if it was vague.

But even so, it was nice to see how much the other Laenites came out to congratulate me on being named the Handmaiden of Ceru. It was an old title, with great importance, and I could only just smile and nod to the other Laenites I didn't know. Before I could get too worried over it, Garrison would distract me, either by asking another question, or telling me another one of his tales.

Oh, Garrison!

My hand flew to my chest, though whether it was to keep it from breaking or breaking free from my chest, I could not say.

I didn't want him to leave.

"Father, I know Ambassador Grollo can stay until summer, if we allow them," I said, trying my best not to plead with him. "He'd mentioned he wouldn't mind a longer visit when I talked with him at the party."

Father Siah shook his head. "Thessa—"

"We have enough room to house them comfortably while they're here," I continued. "And Ceru's said before that we are to be welcoming to strangers."

"To strangers, not aggressors."

"They aren't aggressors," I argued back.

"They bring trouble with them." Father Siah stood up and walked over beside me. He put his arm around my shoulders in what he thought would be a comforting manner, but it only made me bristle. "Thessa, Father Ephyras and the rest of the Priests and Spiritual Mothers have discussed this at some length with Ambassador Grollo. We are in agreement, even if he is not."

"Well, I don't agree, either." I shrugged my way out of Father Siah's embrace. "The Arians haven't been aggressive toward us at all."

"Aggression is only one form of manipulation," Father Siah reminded me. "The Arians might be here to warn us of trouble brewing, but so far we have no trouble with the Katorians."

"But they're killing innocent people!"

"Do you know that for certain? Do you have proof?"

I scowled. "Garrison's mother was killed because of Fuergo, and he did say there was an attack on them at Triumphia. We can't just sit by and say nothing about this."

"But that's all we've heard—it's nothing we've seen for ourselves. We will need to send out scouts and request information. Some of our soldiers have already left for Triumphia, and Father Ephyras is sending out special messengers to senators in Kator. We cannot jump to conclusions. Say we did join with them; your friends on the frontlines would be put at risk."

I went very still, unable to stop the whirlpool of rage and frustration inside of me. I understood what Father Siah was saying, but I still felt as though I was being treated like a child.

"War is complicated, Thessa," Father Siah continued patiently. "Your education on it is lacking—as is your self-control, today."

That only increased my irritation. I was no longer just a Ghost Child; I was Ceru's Handmaiden, and things were changing. Ceru had told me so himself.

"If there's no proof of trouble, why would allowing the Arians to stay be troublesome?" I asked Father Siah. "You are already jumping to conclusions about their intentions, especially when they've given us no reason to doubt them."

"The Arians have no reason to wait for our final answer on the matter. If they are at war, it's better for them to leave and strengthen their own forces." Father Siah rubbed his temples. "There are some things I cannot tell you, as you know. But for now, let's just drop the pretense, shall we?"

"What do you mean?"

"I know you are enjoying the Arians here, especially thanks to that boy you saved. With your promotion as Ceru's Handmaiden, I've noticed you have been in the spotlight of the people much more frequently."

I narrowed my eyes, growing more angry by the minute. Father Siah and the others were purposefully shoving the Arians out of Laena, and now, he was on the verge of accusing me of misconduct. "What does that have to do with anything?"

"I suspect you know what I am talking about," Father Siah said. "You cannot allow yourself to be too attached to power, Thessa—nor can you allow yourself to get too close to Garrison."

"Why not?"

The words escaped me as a small cry, and I hated Father Siah in that moment. I could see all the pity and impatience in his eyes as he looked down at me.

"He might not be the one Ceru has for you," Father Siah reminded me, using his best patronizing tone. "I know that you hope for such a thing, and there are rumors about it, but he hasn't expressed any interest himself, has he? And—"

"Don't tell me what I hope for," I said.

Father's Siah's words suddenly snapped in fierce warning, scorching me. "I have given up more than you could ever imagine to be where I am now, Thessa. I want to protect you. Don't make this difficult for me."

"Let me make it easier on both of us." I shook my head and turned on my heel. It was time to leave. "I hope you will excuse me."

I silently fumed as I headed out the door. *Father Siah just needs proof of everything today, doesn't he?*

And even worse, he was right. I knew Garrison liked me, but he hadn't spoken of marriage or courting, or really anything else outside of his Life Debt to me. As I reached the door, I felt my resolve weaken.

"You're Ceru's Handmaiden!" Father Siah yelled after me. "You carry his Crest, and you've agreed to your fate. You won't escape it now, Thessa."

At Father Siah's anger, my own stirred.

"I've agreed to the fate Ceru's given me," I shouted back. "Not the one that you or the priests or the Spiritual Mothers want for me—or Ceru's people, either."

Father Siah took a deep breath before he spoke again. "Maybe you should talk to Ceru himself before you get too upset over this, Thessa."

I swallowed hard. I had gone to see Ceru, slipping in to see him at night as I usually did. But ever since my Adoption Day, he had remained silent and sleeping.

All I could muster out was a half-hearted, "Maybe I will," before I stormed out of his office and left the Cathedral.

Inside me, a flurry of righteous indignation raged.

Outside, the world was mocking me.

The weather couldn't have been more of a contrast to my mood; it was nearly the first day of spring, and a sweet rush of flowers mixed with anticipation swam all around me as I walked out into town and headed for the harbor. There was a heady scent of springtime coming from the sea and mountains.

My hands were shaking as I stomped down to the courtyard. I thought briefly of going to see Ceru, but I quickly discarded the idea.

He would be nicer, but he would still tell me I'd been wrong to yell at Father Siah, who only wanted the best for me, and the entire tribe, too.

But Father Siah was wrong. I clenched my fist. Father Siah should've supported me—he should've made the arrangements for me to go and talk with their small council of Priests and Spiritual Mothers, or something like that.

And he had no business trying to keep me from Garrison, either.

At the thought of him, I cheered, if only slightly, and I decided to go and seek him out. I didn't have to be at the medic station for a few more hours, and spending the time with Garrison might help me feel better.

I walked toward the harbor, gazing over at the ambassador's ship. There were men there who waved at me as I passed, and I waved back. Other Laenites who saw me called out their greetings to me as well, and I thought back to what Father Siah had said.

Was I getting too enamored of my new-found influence?

The attention was nice, especially after all the years I had been ignored. As I talked to the people, conversations that I would never have had a month ago now came to me without hindrance—especially those regarding the possibility of Laena going to war.

Mothers wringed their hands, anxious over the fate of their children, and wives worried for their husbands. "We're not really going to fight with the Katorians, are we? They're ruthless!"

There were merchants who cheered at the thought of opening more markets, and there were young boys eager to fight for truth and justice. "Do you think we'll get the High Priest to approve opening more trade routes?"

And then there was a collection of youthful optimism and excitement at the thought of war: "Those who do evil will die!"

All of these voices were wrapped up in their hope that I could make a difference, that I could have some sway—and I honestly didn't know what I could even tell them.

It would be nice to have Ceru's thoughts on this matter.

Yes, it would, but he did not seem to be worried about it, or he would've woken up, wouldn't he?

I rubbed my temples, trying to hide my uncertainty; at that moment, it did nothing to help me with the barrage of questions and comments I was receiving.

Finally, I had to excuse myself and, unable to find Garrison, I headed back toward the medic station. I still had several of the people call out to me and try to talk to me, and after a while, I missed how they used to ignore me.

It certainly took less time to get from place to place before I saved Garrison's life and Ceru decreed I was to be his Handmaiden.

I slid toward an empty alleyway, eager for a moment alone. As I stood there, watching the town, I pulled out the Crest of Ceru and studied it.

Despite what Father Siah might've thought, I was proud to be given the honor of being his Handmaiden. The title came with some prestige among my community, even if the duties of it were unclear to me.

I knew I was to help tend to him, but I had always done that. This just seemed to make it official.

But if it was official, shouldn't that mean I become more of an advocate for him, too?

Ceru was getting older. He would sometimes sleep for days at a time, even now; in the last year, I would come and curl up next to him, and he would never bat an eye, even if his tail and his wings would instinctively protect me.

"The Age of Dragons is ending."

My heart nearly stopped. Did that mean Ceru would have to die? And what about the other dragons?

I clutched at the Crest, letting the gemstone in the middle of it press against my heart. I could feel the power inside of it, and I quickly discarded the idea that Ceru would die.

He was the Great Sea Serpent, and the dragon of the healing waters. He would be able to outlive everyone in my community, as he had since his arrival fourteen generations ago.

"Please, Creator," I whispered, ducking my head in desperate prayer. "Protect him and sustain him. Ceru has always been the one I've loved most, and I've always tried to please him."

I opened my eyes and looked up to the sky expectedly, as though I'd get some kind of answer.

That's when I heard Garrison's voice, coming from around the corner.

"Well, Miss Kana, you've certainly proved your worth."

I glanced around the corner to see Garrison was talking with Kana. She flipped her dark hair over her shoulder and gave Garrison a strange smile.

"You know you're welcome to my help anytime," Kana said.

He patted his shoulder, where I could see a small bandage. "I appreciate that, especially given how much my bunkmates like to try to beat me during our battle drills.

Thank the Creator for your healing skills; I doubt I've ever had such a pleasant visit."

My heart sank a little, especially as Kana giggled flirtatiously.

"There's more to me than just a medic. I'm sure there's plenty you would like to see while you're here," she said. "I'd be happy to help you."

Garrison grinned at her. "Well, I haven't been disappointed by our interactions so far," he said. "What did you have in mind?"

At that, my righteous indignation from earlier flared up again, this time much more dangerous.

"Yes, Kana," I called through gritted teeth as I stormed my way over to them. "What did you have in mind?"

I glared at her, and she shrugged, while giving me a haughty look. Without waiting for her answer, I grabbed hold of Garrison's wrist and pulled at him. I was more than happy to leave Kana behind, even though I didn't know if I was entirely happy to be alone with Garrison.

"I've been looking for you," I said, trying to get the anger out of my voice but failing. "It's a good thing I found you. Kana is … just not someone you need to be around."

"Whoa, hold on, Thessa. She wasn't doing anything wrong," Garrison said.

"What?" I rounded on him. "You mean you were the one who started flirting with her?"

"No, of course not," he said with a sigh. "I was just being friendly, Thessa. And so was she. That's all. My father wants me to make a good impression here, and I had a small injury this morning when one of my fellow soldiers accidentally dropped a knife while we were fighting."

He nodded toward his bandage, as if he was pleading for me to have sympathy for him.

"Perhaps I should order you not to talk to her in the future, then," I finally said. "That would get your father on my side in this matter, wouldn't it?"

His lips curled up into that charming smirk I couldn't resist. "You know you're the only person with a credit to themselves here, so far as I'm concerned."

When I only frowned, he reached for my hand and kissed it again, just as he had the previous night.

When he lifted his head back up and saw I was still unamused, Garrison cleared his throat.

"See, it's a joke, right? Because you are the one I owe a Life Debt to, and you are also my favorite person here."

"I am?" I was suspicious of his claim, especially since I had seen how he'd looked at Kana, and how Kana had looked at him.

But Garrison's easy warmth had a way of smoothing over a lot of my doubts.

"Of course you are, Thessa," he said. "From what everyone says, you're very kind, and compassionate, and loving. And I know firsthand of your bravery. I can't think of anyone who would make a better friend."

My waxing enthusiasm cratered. "Friend?"

"Or perhaps more?" Garrison winked at me. "Kana was just offering to take me on a tour of the bay area, but I would much rather you escort me. Do you have some time?"

He didn't wait for my answer, before he took my hand and we started walking toward the port.

My fingers twined naturally around his, and it didn't take me long to realize I'd be late for work.

CHAPTER SEVEN

※ ※ ※ ※

"Ah, this is lovely." I giggled as I waded into the oceanfront.

It was a moment of true freedom. From where Garrison and I were standing, I could see the whole of Cathedral City's harbor was shaped like a crescent behind me with the Cathedral in the heart of the harbor, directly in front of the Hallowed Mountain. Garrison and I were off to one side, just below the mountains, where the rocks seemed to fade down into the waterline like a natural, rocky staircase.

"I agree." Garrison seemed much more relaxed as he took a seat on a large boulder behind me. "From this distance, even my father's eagle eyes would have trouble spotting me."

"It must be nice to have a father, though," I said. "As a Ghost Child, I don't know who my real father is. Or my mother, for that matter."

"Be glad of that," Garrison scoffed. He tried to keep his voice light, but I could feel the sharpness behind it. "My father is always ready to remark on my disappointments, and yet every time I attempt to prove him wrong, he's already prepared to sabotage my efforts."

At that moment, it was all too easy to think of Father Siah and Father Ephyras.

"The truth is, there's very little difference between a parent and a tyrant."

"I wouldn't say that. Your father does seem to care for you," I said.

"Of course he does," Garrison agreed, a little too easily, and when I gave him a pressing look, he sighed. "I am his only true heir," he said. "I have plenty of half-brothers and sisters with his concubines, but only I will inherit his title, his lands, and all his influence. He uses me to increase what he has now, so I can provide for the rest of the family when he's gone."

I waded back over to Garrison, giving myself a moment to think over what he'd admitted.

In the Laenite Tribe, we did not allow for extramarital affairs. Tribe members who abused this were formally exiled from the clan and shunned, especially if there were Ghost Children involved. We kept the children here, so they would be safe, and they would be raised with an education that would hopefully prevent the sins of the family's blood from continuing. The other nations and tribes often dismissed our concern for marriage and family, and as I made my way over to sit next to him, I couldn't help but think how Garrison's troubles might have been avoided.

But knowing they could've been avoided didn't help him now, and as a medic, it was my natural inclination to want to comfort him.

"If your family members are as smart as you, I'm sure they will be able to take care of themselves," I said. "Perhaps they won't be as much of a burden as you think."

"Let us hope so, for their sakes as much as mine." Garrison laughed, just a little too sharply, while I remained quiet and confused.

When he saw the look on my face, he shrugged and looked out toward the Arian ship again. "They'll probably have to participate in the war," he said. "Forgive me if I don't seem too attached to them. The distance between us is necessary, especially if my fear of losing them compromises my judgement."

"But you actually are quite close?" I asked.

Garrison nodded. "Too close for my father's liking," he agreed with a somber look. "I grew up surrounded by them—all six of them. Arians aren't too particular about things the way the Laenites are—as you may know," he said, giving me a small smirk. "But the one thing that they do insist on is bloodline purity. The Arian Kingdom is held together over several islands, and my family's held our lands for the last seven generations. It is up to me to honor that responsibility."

"I envy you that connection," I said. I pulled out the Crest of Ceru and showed it to him. "I have my own responsibility to honor here, as Ceru's Handmaiden. But I know what it feels like to be surrounded by people you want to protect. My friends are like my family."

Garrison nodded. "My siblings were my friends before I found out they were my family, too. War is not kind to either, and if we're going to win the war against the Katorians, I have to grow up and leave such things behind."

"You seem plenty grown up to me." I spoke a little too quickly, and as Garrison flashed me his charming smile, I felt the heat rise in my cheeks.

"I'll be nineteen soon," he said. "My birthday is in another couple of weeks."

I looked back at the water. "I guess you'll be able to celebrate your birthday at home in the Arian Kingdom. You should be back there by then, right?"

"Yes."

His reply was brusque, but I didn't push him to elaborate on his plans. When I said nothing, he leaned forward, putting his elbows on his knees.

"I just realized, this will be the first year I won't have my mother around," he said.

The sadness in his voice made my heart break. I took his hand in mine and held it.

"I'm sorry," I said. "I'm sure she was very proud of you."

"Well, that's not going to help me much now," he said, pulling back from me. "And as nice as you are, Thessa, you're not really going to be able to help me, either."

"I can't bring your mother back," I said slowly, "but I can help in other ways, perhaps?"

"No, you can't," Garrison scoffed. He stood up and brushed back his dark blond hair. The mist in the air had darkened it, but the sun made it shimmer. He was breathtakingly beautiful, even in his anger. "My father's already told me that the High Priest and the council here won't help us fight the Katorians."

"I know," I admitted. "Father Siah told me that we don't have enough proof. That's the downside of being up here, on top of the world. We are fairly self-sufficient, and we aren't bothered by the rest of the world very often."

"If the Katorians are fighting with us at Triumphia, you can believe they'll make their way up here next," Garrison said. "Maybe they'll even do it in a nice way, sending someone harmless-looking up here to warn you about us."

I smiled. "We wouldn't believe that."

"Cathedral City's council might."

"Well, I wouldn't," I insisted, standing up next to him. "I know we haven't known each other long, but I would trust your word over theirs in a heartbeat."

Garrison paused and looked me over, making me blush profusely. "Is that so?" he finally asked, and I nodded, too embarrassed to say anything.

And then he walked over to me and took both my hands, squeezing them tightly.

"You're right when you say we haven't known each other long," Garrison said. "But there is a connection I feel with you, Thessa, and I don't think it's just because you've saved my life."

My tongue felt too thick to say anything, so I just nodded and smiled, trying not to stare at his full lips.

But instead, he eased away from me, clearly hesitant.

"The Arians are a kingdom dedicated to beauty," he said slowly. "We don't really worship Aria the way you do with Ceru here. So perhaps the reason I like you so much is because you remind me that there's an element of goodness that's required for beauty."

"Perhaps that is the answer we need for the war," I whispered. "Goodness and beauty, truth and love, united together in the face of unholy fire."

"Unity?" Garrison looked a little uneasy. "What do you mean?"

I squared my shoulders, trying to look confident, even if I didn't feel it. "The Age of Dragons is ending," I said. "Ceru told me so himself."

"Well, war is inevitable then," Garrison said with a sigh. "The Dragons are the ones who rule over us. Without them, there would be a power vacuum. Fuergo's people must already know this. That is why the Katorian Republic attacks my kingdom."

"The Creator sent us the Dragon Guardians to help us live peaceful and holy lives," I said, remembering the Laenite Tribe's teachings on the matter. "Perhaps war would be our judgment in failing to do that."

"You think we deserve war?" Garrison asked, his voice much sharper and angrier than ever before. "You think it was good that my mother died and the rest of my family is now in danger?

"No, no, of course not," I quickly assured him. "I was just thinking, war is what will come, if we don't act—if we don't unite in the face of this coming change."

"Your tribe has already made their position clear."

"But *we* can still do something," I said. "We can get married."

"Married?"

Garrison's face was so stupefied, I almost laughed.

But it was perfect—and it was that simple.

"Yes," I said. "As Ceru's Handmaiden, I am the one who tends to him directly. I am also one of the few people in the tribe who can get Ceru to give me Dragon Tears, which help heal even the worst of wounds. If you marry me, you can have an alliance with the Laenites based on love and respect."

"I see," Garrison said slowly. He rubbed his chin. "Even if the Laenites wouldn't fight with the Katorians, we would have the advantage in treating our wounded."

"Well—"

"You can promise me this?" Garrison asked. "And you would marry me, to do this for me?"

"Of course." I blushed, caught off guard by his question as much as my response. I hadn't even had the chance to tell Garrison about the child I would have, and how I would give birth to the future ruler of the dragonlands. But as he looked at me, I decided not to worry about that now. He seemed eager to protect his family, and that was something we could agree on, and it was something that I felt could earn his love. "I've already saved your life. I might as well try to save others', as well."

"Oh, Thessa." Garrison ran up to me and grabbed me, before twirling me around in a high circle. "You really are too good to be true, aren't you?"

Before I could answer him, he pulled me down close and pressed his lips against mine in an earth-shattering kiss.

The sea's mist added an intoxicating saltiness to his kiss I wasn't expecting, and before I knew it, I was clinging to him in return, desperate and fumbling to keep him close.

He finally set my feet down on the ground again. "I'll have to inform my father at once," he said. "You and I can do this, right, Thessa?"

I put my fingers up to my lips, dazzled by the kiss he'd given me. "Yes," I said, pushing back all thoughts of Father Siah's earlier warnings. "Yes, we can do this."

CHAPTER EIGHT

※ ※ ※ ※

In the Present ...

Thunder roars loudly around me. My heart beats erratically as I wake up, and I gasp loudly in surprise and fear as I sit up. My head is splitting with pain, as though it had snapped in two along with my heart.

"No," I whisper, though I am alone and well into the Laenite mountains by now. My voice is scratchy and dry from two days on the run, despite the past two days of overcast skies and the drizzling rain.

I roll over onto my side, and then reluctantly push myself up. I shake out my robes, and push back my hair, which seems to have lost its golden luster. My tongue is thick and my breath is sour, and I wish I could curl back down in the small, mostly-dry hovel I'd found the night before and go back to sleep.

But I know I won't be able to get back to sleep.

It is better for me to keep moving.

Even in the dark, even in the rain, even in the thunder.

I do my best to walk steadily, even though my head pounds with the additional pain of unshed tears, and my only hope is in making it to the Great Waterfall.

I couldn't be more than a few hours away from the waterfall at the edge of Laena. It is getting closer, and I am leaving my past shame behind.

Garrison.

I remember his sweet and salty kiss on the small beach by Cathedral City Harbor.

I trace my lips, trying to relive that moment of my life. It had been so happy and wonderous.

So unlike my life and everything that happened afterward.

The sun is not yet up in the sky, but there is enough early morning light I can make my way through the heavy forest without issue. A rueful smirk curls on my lips, wondering cynically if this was to help compensate for the last two years of my life.

My steps slow down ever so slightly as I think of all the disapproval I had to face down once Garrison and I announced our intent to wed to our respective communities.

Ambassador Grollo was full of excitement, especially after Garrison told him it would allow the Arians to bring their wounded to Laena for treatment.

I stumble, but I catch myself before I fall. My knee still hurts from the other night when I escaped the Hallowed Mountain, but I ignore the crackle in my joints.

All my problems will be over soon.

Garrison ... I should have seen this coming ... why didn't I see it?

It was too easy to see the answer now. I had built Garrison up to be a prince among men, and I had never seen him for his true self, all the good and all the bad.

It was just so complicated.

Just like everything else.

Father Ephyras and Ambassador Grollo worked out a nice deal; once Father Ephyras knew Laena would be greatly compensated for our assistance—especially when the senators from Kator sent back notices announcing the Arians were formally at war with Kator—he approved my engagement.

It bothered me how he seemed to like the idea of getting money while being connected to the Arian Kingdom's army. But I felt a little better when Father Ephyras insisted that the Arians train with our soldiers, who had never truly seen a war, so we would be better able to protect our homes.

The Laenite Tribe began taking in the Arians who were wounded in battle, as Fuergo's Katorian forces began attacking them almost as soon as my engagement to Garrison was finalized.

Garrison, as a result, wasn't around Laena much, and while we communicated through letters, it was a poor substitute. I didn't even feel like they were written by him, since they sounded so professional and informative, especially when compared to the passion and promise that filled each of mine.

It didn't help he was about my only hope left, as the war took Edmun and Davar on tours around the island, and Pia and Philia were left working longer hours to help with the families who had soldiers on tour. This was another reason my friends, along with others, were more upset with me, too.

Even Ceru seemed content to let me suffer.

Ceru.

That was the worst part of all—worse than the war between the Arians and the Katorians, the distance between me and Garrison, and the growing distance between me and the rest of the Laenite Tribe.

When Ceru had said he would talk to me after the end of my Life Debt, when I turned seventeen, he apparently meant it.

He fell asleep after giving me the Crest, and he never really woke up again. He did a little, at times, but only grumbled out simple answers, frustrating Father Ephyras to no end.

Father Siah remained practical to the end—although I suspect now that it was his desired end.

"There is no way you can get married without Ceru's approval," he told me. "You will have to wait until your seventeenth Adoption Day, in this case."

Father Siah was perfectly happy delaying my wedding, but I actually agreed with a smile, frustrating him in return.

I was happy that the community would be made aware of my wedding, and I would have plenty of time to plan it. I could order things from Aria, I could have food shipped in from around the world, I could request their choir make up a new song, just for me and Garrison. There was so much to do, and even though there was a war happening, I didn't seem to notice it outside of the medic station.

My stomach growls at the thought of food.

I put my hand over it to steady myself, but as my palms flatten against my stomach, I finally stop walking.

My hand stays on my stomach, rubbing it in a mindless sort of fashion, the way I had seen countless mothers do in the past.

I think back to the child of prophecy I had been promised.

If there was anything I would cry over, despite my vow against Ceru, it would be my baby—the baby Garrison and I would never have now.

The raindrops transform into mist and the thunder coils downstream as I stand here, and my hands tremble as I hear the rushing sound of freedom ahead of me.

The Great Waterfall.

I look ahead and I see the crystal beacon of the riverfront ahead of me. I start to feel the fog of the water, wafting up all around me. I can taste the saltiness in the air.

It is a bittersweet thing, to stand here, at the edge of my home, willing to forsake everything.

Every memory.

Every hope.

Every dream.

My hand is shaking again as I raise it up to reach the Crest, still hanging around my neck.

I clench the amulet in my fist, suddenly more defiant and powerful than ever as I feel its power beat against my palm.

The weather and the world around me wanted to break me, to make me cry.

But I am done.

Ceru had told me himself that I knew the power of tears, and that also meant I knew the power of resisting them.

After all the years of loneliness and longing, after all the changes and the plans and the hardship, the small moments of celebration that only seemed to make everything even more disappointing in the end …

After all of that, I will not allow myself to cry anymore.

Not after what had happened. Not after what he did to me.

CHAPTER NINE

※ ※ ※ ※

A Week Before ...

I woke up to my seventeenth Adoption Day feeling excitement like never before.

Today's the day!

I hopped out of bed like a lightning bolt out of the clouds, and hurried to get ready. I was going to see Ceru today, and by midday, I would be married.

By this time, I'd gotten used to Ceru's relative silence and sleepiness, and while I still alternated between being anxious for his health and irritated at his distance, I still believed everything with Garrison would work out as I'd planned.

So far, everything else seemed to be going well enough.

The healers in the medic station were helping the fallen Arians, and we were even able to remind some of the more hedonistic ones of the Creator's call for holiness, mercy, and forgiveness, encouraging them to seek out our religious comfort in the Cathedral.

My friends, in seeing the fruits of their labors, came to agree with me that it had been a good move to work with the Arians and take in their injured and ill. Pia was learning how to be her own chef from an Arian sailor she'd befriended in her free time, and I was more than certain Philia and Davar were using an Arian messenger service to write love letters to each other. Edmun had just returned with Garrison from a meeting with the Arian King, himself, and he was full of excitement at having been able to experience such a thing.

To be honest, I was a little jealous of Edmun; I was required, as Ceru's Handmaiden, to stay in Laena until my Life Debt was over. That was thanks to Father Ephyras, but I had a feeling Father Siah was also insistent on keeping me here. I would've loved to go off with Garrison on some of his trips, myself.

It was the day I had waited for ever since the ink had dried on my engagement agreement, and even before that, it was the day I would be let out of my Life Debt to Ceru.

I practically hopped out of bed, excited at the thought, barely realizing it had been ages since I'd gone down to see Ceru.

I paused while I grabbed my navy-colored robes; I had been eager for the last day of winter to be over, and then it occurred to me that I hadn't seen Ceru since I'd checked to see if he was awake in autumn, when I'd been wearing the violet-blue robes the Ghost Children used during that time of year.

Nearly three months, and I hadn't checked on him.

"Has it really been so long?" I wondered aloud to myself.

Yes.

In the pulsating silence of my room, I could hear my guilt echo back my answer to me.

Quickly, I brushed my shame aside. The war between the Arians and the Katorians was harder for us than we'd thought; we didn't send soldiers into battle overseas, but occasionally one of our men would get hurt, too, helping stock up the Arian ships that came into harbor, or working to unload the sick patients into our medic stations. It wasn't easy work for all of our men, especially the older ones like Zebedee, who'd wound up in my care twice with a sprained shoulder.

So of course I would be distracted.

And there was also the matter of planning my wedding.

Which was today, I reminded myself with a smile. I would meet Father Ephyras at the balcony with Garrison, and after Ceru spoke with me and gave his approval, we would head to the sanctuary in the Cathedral.

"That is all we have to do," I whispered, brushing my hair out to its fullest golden shine. I looked in the small mirror in my room, carefully adjusting the Crest of Ceru so it was perfectly centered against my heart and its gemstone reflected light into my own blue eyes.

"Garrison will love this," I whispered, tucking a stray lock of hair behind my ear. It had been a few weeks since his last visit, and I wanted to make sure he was pleased when he saw me again.

I headed out the door. Briefly, I looked back and gave a wistful sigh.

This was the day I had wanted. This was the day when *I* would be wanted; I would finally have a real home of my own, and I would have a family to love me.

Glancing down at my belly, I wondered how long it would be before Garrison and I would have the child Ceru promised.

"Surely not long," I murmured, although I hoped it would be long enough that we would be able to find a good home and settle in. Garrison and I were to spend the first few weeks together in one of the extra guest rooms the Cathedral had, and I think this was for more than my peace of mind. Father Siah had been praying and fasting so much in the last few weeks, he'd lost quite a bit of weight, and it seemed he'd aged at least a decade.

I passed by the door to Father Siah's rooms and paused.

Should I let him know I'm awake?

Garrison and I were supposed to meet with Father Siah, Father Ephyras, and Ceru together before the wedding ceremony. As I looked at his door, I chewed on my bottom lip for a long moment.

And then I decided to go and find Garrison instead.

I'd had a lifetime's worth of Father Siah's company, and I was too eager to embrace more time with Garrison for the next lifetime.

I practically skipped all the way down to the harbor, where Garrison's ship was docked. His father had offered to host us at his small palace in the Arian Islands in a few weeks, and since he was still working with King Cressando on the war efforts, he would not be coming to our wedding today.

I didn't mind so much; there was still an impressive number of Arian diplomats and travelers who had come to see Garrison and me, and nearly everyone who could come from Cathedral City would be there.

As I passed through the streets, I got a few smiles and waves, but most people saw me now and turned away. The response to aiding the Arians had been divisive, even if we were doing well with it. But there were rumors I'd fought for our support of the Arians, and some even said I was too blinded by Garrison, only for his good looks, to see I was bringing us into a war with the other nations.

I kept my chin up, despite everything.

I knew the truth. I was marrying Garrison because I loved him.

And so far, for the past two years, nothing bad had come of our helping the Arians. It was a great blessing to be able to save the lives of the soldiers who came to us.

It wasn't until I saw Pia duck away from me that I slowed.

"Pia!" I called out.

She turned around and waved. "Hi, Thessa," she called. "I've got a busy day today. I'm getting your feast ready, remember? So I can't talk, sorry."

I walked over to her. "Is there anything I can help you with?"

"No, just get ready. It's your big day, right?" She gave me a quick smile, even though she didn't quite look me in the eye.

"Pia, what's wrong?" I asked, taking her arm. "You're not mad at me, are you?"

She twisted out of my reach at once. "By the shadows, Thessa, leave me alone. I'm not mad at you, but Philia is, and even though we are your best friends, today's not a good day for you to pretend you can fix everything."

"What do you mean by that?" I crossed my arms. "Things are different from what they were two years ago, but that doesn't mean it's bad."

"It's not bad for you," Pia snapped. "You've been given a lot of attention and people here mostly like how you tend to the medic station and advocate against injustice. But it's starting to grate on my nerves, especially since Ceru's gone silent."

"That's not my fault," I shot back. "He's been tired and he's getting old, Pia."

"Some people believe he's like that because you're neglecting him."

"I haven't been," I insisted, even though I knew she was at least a little right. "He started sleeping after my Adoption Day, but only because he gave me this."

I pointed to the amulet on my chest.

Pia sighed. "Well, even if it's not your fault, you've been doing all this stuff, and you haven't even thought of how Philia feels."

"About what? She was promoted in her job recently."

"But she's been waiting to hear about her own marriage," Pia said. "She was hoping Davar would hear something when he had his seventeenth Adoption Day."

I held out my hands in front of me apologetically. "I can't control that. Father

Ephyras is still the one who has to approve marriages. He has asked for some others, but not for Philia."

"Well, make him!" Pia rolled her eyes. "Goodness, Thessa. Did it really take me to tell you how to fix this?"

"I've been preoccupied."

"Well, there are more people in the world than you and Garrison."

"I'm going to see Ceru today, right after I meet with Garrison," I said. "I'll ask Father Siah about it, too."

"All right. Thank you." Pia shook her head and put her hand on her hip. "I'm sure Philia will be happy to hear you'll be her advocate, and please know I love you as a dear friend. But I do really have to get to your feast."

"I'm looking forward to seeing what you've made." I did my best to smile brightly at her, but I was relieved when we awkwardly waved goodbye.

I shook off my discomfort a moment later. There was a lot more activity around the harbor this morning, and Pia was likely just as much right about the stress she faced today as she was about Philia's anger at me.

But I said I would help, didn't I? And I had tried to make amends. And I would make sure that even though I was getting married today, I would be better to my friends in the coming weeks, to help make up for any discomfort I'd inadvertently caused, I vowed.

And then everything would be perfect; everything would work out, just as I wanted.

As if to agree with me, I looked up and saw Garrison coming down the gangway plank of his ship.

Never had I seen such a glorious man, I thought. As a fifteen-year-old, I'd been enchanted by Garrison's good looks, and each time I'd seen him over the past two years, it had seemed he'd only gotten more handsome.

His dark blond hair was a little longer than when I'd first met him, but there was a spark in his gray-green eyes that I could see across the port. He was wearing the silver armor of the Arian forces, with a special cobalt lining that marked him as a messenger.

He came up to me and took a knee, bowing over my hand.

"My lovely Handmaiden, Thessa," he said in greeting, before giving my hand a quick kiss. "I am here at last. Nothing seems to be right but to be here in your service."

He was still his charming self, and I knelt down next to him and kissed him, surprising him.

"It's been a few months," I said, giggling a little as I saw the stunned look on his face.

He brushed back his hair and shrugged. "No bother," he replied easily. "Now, are we to go and see your dragon today, at last?"

"Yes." I took Garrison by the arm and tugged him after me. "I can't wait for you to meet him."

"He's always been here, inside the Hallowed Mountain?" Garrison asked, looking around.

"Yes, that's his home. There's a special hallway in the Cathedral that takes you down to his nest under the mountain. It's got a lovely stream that flows through the land, all the way back to the Great Waterfall that marks our Southern border," I explained.

"I hope he will like me."

I was surprised by the genuine concern in his voice.

"I'm sure he will love you," I said softly, wanting to reassure and encourage my future husband. "I know I do."

Garrison nodded somberly, before his usual smirk was back. "Well, I'm hoping that I can get some goodwill on my own. Not just from being your life slave for the past two years."

"Oh, that reminds me," I said. "While we're with Ceru, I will have to release you from that. No one who gets married is allowed to be in a Life Debt with another."

"Oh?" Garrison looked around the town, no doubt taking in the decorations and grandeur that the Laenites and the Arians had collectively built. "I actually thought it was mostly just a joke. I mean, I was happy to go along with it, but you don't need Ceru to be present to take it away, do you?"

"That's the way I've always assumed it was done." I frowned, thinking it over. I'd never seen anyone but the Ghost Children be released from a Life Debt. But I did know one of the Priests or the Spiritual Mothers were usually present. So it was likely similar to an adoption or a marriage. "Either way, it's best we take care of it. I will be free of my Life Debt to Ceru today, too."

"Interesting." Garrison was still looking around at the town, and I thought he seemed a little uncomfortable as he looked around.

Perhaps it was wedding day shadows? I'd heard of them before. It was a life-changing experience.

I decided not to worry about it.

By the time Garrison and I arrived down in Ceru's nest, on the same balcony where I'd received the Crest two years before, I'd forgotten all about it.

Ceru was awake.

"Ceru!" I called excitedly, eager to see the dragon I'd loved and who'd loved me back all my life. "You're awake."

"Thessa." Ceru came to the balcony's edge, letting his long neck reach down so I could put my cheek against his while Father Siah and Father Ephyras looked on. I tried not to notice how old and tired Ceru looked. There were white patches down his back where he'd failed to molt into a new set of dragon scales, and the normal blue of his skin had blurred into gray.

As I hugged him, I could almost feel the inner light inside of him grow dim. I swallowed hard, suddenly unsure he would live much longer.

He'll be all right, I thought, still determined to believe all things would work out for my good, and others' too.

I pulled back from him, but I still held onto his cheeks. "A lot has happened since you last woke up like this," I said, struggling to keep my voice from breaking.

"Nothing has happened that will change the outcome, nor shall such a thing happen now," Ceru told me. His large, luminous eyes looked behind me. *"I see you've brought a suitor for me."*

"Yes," I whispered excitedly. "I knew you would like him. I knew he had to be the one. Otherwise, you would've told me. Or you would've said something to one of the Fathers, here, anyway, and I know how much they would've liked that at times."

Ceru nuzzled me softly. *"Is this the one you would choose, Thessa?"*

"Yes," I whispered, looking back at Garrison. I frowned to see he'd scuttled back several steps from me, and he was looking at me and Ceru with fear in his eyes.

"Are you talking to it?" he asked, and just at that moment, I cringed. I was about to apologize for Garrison when Ceru spoke to me again.

"What if I have someone better for you?" Ceru asked.

"Huh?" I chuckled. "Oh, Ceru, there's no one better for me than Garrison here."

Ceru slowly blinked as he watched Garrison. Father Siah came up behind him and put an arm on his shoulder and whispered something in his ear.

It was nice Father Siah was on my side, I thought. I was truly grateful for it, too, as Garrison straightened up and bowed to Ceru in greeting.

"Let me talk to him." Ceru gently nudged me aside, and then stood tall himself.

"Garrison, Ceru would like to talk to you." I walked over and took him by the arm again, pulling him up after me.

"Let him walk on his own, Thessa," Father Ephyras said. "He's a grown man, after all."

"Yes, Father." I gritted my teeth through the response, but I felt better when Father Siah came to stand between us.

As Garrison stood before Ceru, I watched as he nodded and gave a few responses, but I couldn't make out what he was saying. I glanced up at Father Siah, who nodded.

"This is always how it is," he said. "Some words are not meant for others to hear."

"I see," I whispered back. "What do you think Ceru is talking to him about?"

"I'm sure we will find out soon enough," Father Siah said. There was a sad smile on his face. "There are some things that are better if people don't know, but if it is important for them to know, the truth will come out in the end."

He gave me another one of his patronizing pats on the shoulder. I shrugged it off, before remembering my promise to Pia.

"Father Siah, would you be able to talk to Ceru after this?" I asked. "I wanted to see if Ceru would agree to let Philia and Davar get married, too. She's been waiting while he's been asleep."

"I can ask him, Thessa, but there are still other matters Father Ephyras and I have to discuss with him, such as—"

"My wedding."

"Your wedding, the war—"

"What do you need to ask him about for the war?"

"Thessa—" Father Siah gave me one of his exasperated looks, but before he could say anything else, Garrison let out a sharp gasp.

"No," he grunted, stepping back from Ceru. "No, it's not true."

"Garrison?" I took a tentative step forward.

Before I could get a clear answer from him, Garrison turned away from Ceru. His face, usually glistening from the sun, was ashen.

"Garrison?" I reached forward, but he stepped back from me and shook his head. "What is it?"

"Nothing," he muttered. "Just … I am feeling a bit cramped in here, in this cave. Forgive me, I must leave."

I couldn't stop him from running away. "Garrison!"

"Thessa, you must wait," Father Ephyras said. "Ceru has more for you, remember? Your Life Debt must be addressed."

I looked from Ceru, who was still his old and sad-looking self, to Garrison's fleeing form, and then to Father Siah's resigned look. With begrudging acceptance, I walked back up toward Ceru, and Father Ephyras began to recite a passage from our holy books, one that honored the completion of a Life Debt.

"What did you say to Garrison, Ceru?" I whispered, as Father Ephyras continued to pontificate.

"I told him the truth about your baby," Ceru said. *"And also that he can be forgiven for the pain he causes me, but not for the pain he inflicts on you."*

"What? What did you say? Garrison wouldn't hurt me. Were you warning him away from me?" I asked, turning my full attention on Ceru. I frowned. "I've already told him about the baby, too. I hope you don't mind; I thought he would like that. He's very dedicated to his family."

“Thessa, pay attention,” Father Ephyras hissed. “This is the end of the passage, and I need your response.”

“Sorry.” I flickered my gaze back to Ceru, who only blinked in that achingly slow way.

Has Ceru gone mad, after all these long years? I glanced back up the stairs, looking to see if Garrison was waiting for me at the top.

There was no sign of him.

“Thessa?”

I sighed and turned my attention back to Father Ephyras. “Yes, Father?”

“Did you hear me? I need you to say if you are in agreement. Do you agree to end your Life Debt with Ceru, the Great Sea Serpent, the Water Dragon Guardian of the Laenite Tribe?”

I nodded quickly. “Yes, I do.”

“Then I pronounce your debt as paid in full,” Father Ephyras said. “You are no longer under the bondage of a Life Debt.”

“Thank you.” I reached over and hugged Ceru. “And thank you. I wouldn’t have made it without you.”

Ceru leaned into my hug. *"I have always loved you, Thessa, as your father loved you. He would have done anything to make sure you were safe."*

"My father loved me?" I don't know why I was so surprised to hear the news I'd been loved.

"Yes. In three days' time, you will begin to see what I mean as you become the mother of the Dragon Lord."

"I'll become pregnant this week?" I asked, suddenly horrified. "But there's so much to do for the wedding still."

Ceru looked toward Garrison's departure, and then nudged me affectionately. *"Everything will be done, according to the will of the Creator, Thessa. As you have trusted and loved me, so you should trust and love him. I am only his servant. Promise me you will remember."*

"Thank you," I whispered again, unable to stop myself from tearing up. "I will remember, I promise."

As I left the Hallowed Mountain, I thought about how I loved Ceru's kindness. He loved me, and he loved me enough to provide for me, and then let me go on and love someone else. There were some Ghost

Children who volunteered to stay under their Life Debt, serving as Priests and Spiritual Mothers; there were others who chose that life later on, too, but I thought about how easily Ceru could've asked me to give up my dreams of getting married and having a family to find contentment in serving him at the Cathedral.

I waved goodbye to Ceru, who weakly turned away and headed back toward his nest. I heard the water splash wildly as he made his careless steps, but I didn't stop running out of the Hallowed Mountain.

I had to find Garrison and then we had to get married.

How else would the child of prophecy be born?

At the thought of that, I smiled. And my smile only grew brighter as I headed toward the Cathedral sanctuary, where Garrison and I were scheduled to be wed in another hour's time.

It was only as I stood waiting for Garrison to show up at the Cathedral ten minutes after we were to be wed that I started to lose my smile.

And then it was twenty minutes after that when I lost my smile completely.

CHAPTER TEN

※ ※ ※ ※

"Garrison! Garrison Rico, come out of your ship right now, you coward!"

No one had to tell me I looked like a desperate fool. I was standing on the port, much like the day I had met Garrison—only this time I was wearing my special, one of a kind, Arian-designed wedding gown, and a matching crown of flowers on my head. It was already starting to come apart as I left the Cathedral, and the run down to the port did nothing to help it. I was sweating and there was plenty of dust kicked up onto my dress, and my fancy shoes were full of dirt.

If Garrison fell off the ship this time, I wouldn't be able to save him.

If I would even want to save him.

"Garrison!" I was watching his crew pack up the ship in a hurry. The twenty minutes I'd spent waiting in the sanctuary were the purest form of torture I'd ever endured, standing before all the people I'd grown up with, waiting for my groom to come and wed me, only to find out from

Davar that Garrison was planning on leaving port immediately.

"What?" I felt the blood drain from my face as Davar told me what he'd seen.

"I also heard him tell his crew they were going to meet with his father in Triumphia," Davar said. "He apparently had to discuss some new developments with him."

I couldn't get past the part where Garrison was leaving.

"Oh, Thessa, I'm so sorry," Philia said, coming up and hugging me as the whispers around us increased along with the crowd's impatience. I heard a familiar giggle behind me, only to see Kana was there, looking more flawless than usual.

"Poor Thessa," she said, trying to hide her obvious glee at my misfortune. "I'm sure he's just terrified to be wed to someone as … blessed … as you."

I *almost* hit her for that.

Instead, I squared my shoulders. "I'll go see what's keeping him," I snapped, glaring at the crowd, daring any one of them to tell me I was wrong.

No one had such gumption—or if they did, they were determined to let me suffer from my own actions.

After running down to the port, I looked all around, fervently praying I would find Garrison and we could get everything sorted out before everything went irrevocably wrong.

"Garrison, don't do this to me!" I yelled. "I saved your life, remember? You owe me that much."

There was a moment of silence before I saw Garrison reluctantly peer out of a nearby building. He'd been overseeing the last of the few cargo shipments when I'd come to the port, screaming.

"Thessa."

At the look on his face, I didn't want to hear him say anything. I knew he was only going to say things that would hurt to hear.

"No, no," I whimpered. "Why are you doing this to me?"

"Look, Thessa, I'm sorry, but I can't do this," Garrison said. "There's too much at stake, really. I mean, my father's just sent word that he needs help in Triumphia, and I just gotta take my soldiers here and go, you know?"

"You're lying," I snapped. "I can tell when you lie."

"You can?" Garrison's usually charming face fell flat. "Well, damn it all to hell, then."

I blinked at his cursing. He'd never cursed in front of me before.

"See?" He pointed at me. "You don't know me as well as you thought you did."

"We will get to know each other after we get married," I insisted, trying to cover up my discomfort. "And if you love me, you will think about how to show me the value of your love."

"Thessa … " Garrison sighed. "Look, I do love you. You're a very lovely girl. You are sweet and thoughtful and you are eager to take care of people. I can see why Ceru wants you to be the future Dragon Lord's mother. But I don't love you the way—or anywhere near the amount—that you love me. Or some illusion of me that you've imagined to be real these past two years."

For a long moment, I just stared at him. "I don't understand," I said. "I know you well enough. We've spent hours talking—"

"Yes, about the war, and the Arian's efforts to get justice for killing my mother,"

Garrison agreed. "My father was so glad when we hit it off in the beginning. He was even willing to forgive me for playing around on the deck and making a spectacle of myself at our arrival here, with the flute and everything. And then you did such a wonderful job, helping us gain the Laenite aid and support for the war. I mean, really, marrying you would've even been fine for political purposes, but Ceru's requirements are just too much of a price for me and my father and our family to pay. So I must kindly, and regretfully, decline."

"You can't just leave me, though," I said, as Garrison started to back away from me, much as he'd backed away from Ceru before. "We can talk about this, can't we?"

"I'm sorry, Thessa. I have to leave. Trust me, it's better this way. Good luck with Ceru's baby." He hesitated again. "I *am* really sorry."

He almost extended his hand for me to shake, before he thought better of it, and simply bowed. I stood there, paralyzed by a brokenness I'd never felt so deeply.

I was still trying to process his words as Edmun came up beside me and tried to get me to move. I was crying too hard to see anything by that point, and I had to be helped every step of the way from the port to my room.

It was the most humiliating moment of my life, and I lived through it again and again and again for the next several days, as I stayed in my room, delirious and depressed.

Every whisper and every sideways look I could imagine hit me, slicing through my heart as medics came and helped me.

I don't know how long it was before I stood up, dressed myself so calmly, and then made my way back to Ceru's nest.

He was back in the center of it, but when I appeared on the balcony—not in my usual spot, sleeping under his wings, he seemed to sense the urgency of the situation.

"Thessa."

"You knew he was going to say no, didn't you?"

I practically spat out the question at Ceru. Over the past few days, every ounce of rage had boiled inside of me, waiting for a chance to escape, waiting until I found the perfect target.

And I found it.

This was all Ceru's fault.

I did everything else right. I stood up for the foreigner, provided care to the injured. I advocated for peaceful means of helping and cooperation among different nations.

And I did it all knowing I would be rewarded with the man I loved.

But that was too much for Ceru, clearly, and I did not hesitate to say so.

Ceru blinked slowly. *"Garrison Rico is not someone who loves you for your full value, Thessa. He is not willing to die for you."*

"You threatened to kill him?" I gasped, horrified by the thought. "Well, no wonder he left me at the altar then!"

I fell to my knees, already crying again.

"He was the one I wanted to marry," I shouted. "Why couldn't you just give me that? It was the only thing I've really ever wanted."

"Would you really want to be married to a man who wouldn't die for you? And what of your child, Thessa?"

"I don't want to hear about it anymore," I yelled, suddenly heartbroken all over again.

My child. My son or daughter was gone now. I would never have Garrison's child, and I wept even harder at that realization.

"You will bear the one who will unite the Dragonlands. The Age of Dragons is dying, Thessa, along with me."

I stopped crying long enough to look up at him. I turned away again almost immediately, not wanting to see the proof he was right. Ceru's eyes were dim, his movements were sluggish, and the brightness I remembered from before was all but diminished.

"The Dragon Lord will rule over all the lands and unite them as the dragons die, and the wars come to an end."

He sniffed a little, as if somewhat amused. *"Wars have to start first, as the Arians and the Katorians have demonstrated."*

"That has nothing to do with me," I insisted. "Why are you punishing me for the world's sins?"

"I know this is painful," he said in that voiceless way of his. *"But you heard him yourself. He won't take care of you at the cost of himself, let alone the child you will*

bear for me—the child that now grows inside of you."

"I have no child." At that lie, so outrageously bold and silly, I stood up.

There was no way I could be pregnant. Not after Garrison rejected me.

"That's enough," I said. "I'm done. I'll never do anything for you ever again. You've hurt me. This is all your fault, and I can't believe you've ever really loved me after all of this."

"Of course I love you." He moved to place his cheek against my head, but at his touch, I pull away. *"And no matter what, I always will."*

Epilogue

※ ※ ※ ※

In the Present ...

The Great Waterfall roars into my ears as I stand at its top. Before me, I see nothing but the northern forests of Kator, with their tall trees looming over thick and murky shadows.

At last, I have reached my destination.

Ceru's Crest is still in my hand, and I take one last look at it. I touch the gemstone carefully, watching it flicker with light, even though the sky is cluttered with clouds.

"I loved you," I whisper, pushing into my heart's greatest wound and channeling all the power of my wounded pride. "Yet you denied me the one thing I wanted most."

Deep betrayal, unforgettable anger, and unrelenting shame course through me as I think of Garrison's expression as he left the Hallowed Mountain.

Everything I'd ever believed had been upended by Garrison's rejection. I'd been ridiculed and ignored by my Community; I'd been abandoned by the man I'd thought would love me forever. Was it possible that there wasn't a Creator at all?

I put the amulet back under my robes.

I am ready.

And with that, I jump.

I jump off the rocky shelf, sliding into the waterfall's stream, letting the air rush past me.

A scream escapes me as I fall, but I quickly shut my mouth and close my eyes; I wait to plunge into the river below, hoping for a quick end. Perhaps I will fall into a large boulder, or hit a patch of shallow water …

I fall, and then think no more on these things. I think of Garrison who left me, I think of my friends who are likely still out looking for me; I think of Father Siah, and how he would react to the news I was dead; briefly, I wonder who my father is, and how he would feel knowing I would throw all his sacrifice away on my defiant indulgence here; and then I think of Ceru and all his kindnesses, and the baby I would never meet, but wanted to so badly …

I think of all of these things as I hit the water's surface and fall through; there are no rocks to meet me, no shallow ponds to greet me.

I am left to drown under the weight of my robes, and Ceru's Crest.

And after a long moment, I decide this is how it was truly meant to be.

There's a melody that reaches out to me, one as lovely as Garrison's performance on the Arian ship that brought him to me. I can almost hear the angelic forces humming along with it, even though there are no words; it's almost like the song I'd imagined I'd write for Ceru, all those years and months ago.

Funny how I'd forgotten that until now.

I reach out, as if to capture the song, and it whirls around me, the music swelling as I fall further into everlasting darkness, and pass on into the light.

I can feel Ceru's spirit beside me as I close my eyes and allow myself to slip deeper into the waiting arms of death.

And then I am pulled back by something—or someone.

Someone is calling out to me.

"I got you!"

There is a muffled voice yelling at me, as this someone grabs my wrist, pulls me up out of Ceru's song, and frees my body out from the river.

I feel myself cough before I realize I am coughing; my chest aches and my mouth burns as I spit the water out.

I am more than weak, my body is limp, my clothes are weighed down, all while Ceru's Crest is anchored around my neck.

I don't have to open my eyes to know the truth.

I am not dead.

Why am I still alive?

I had been ready for death, and I'd even thought I'd embraced it.

That was all I wanted after everything that happened—after Ceru's betrayal, Garrison's loss, and my universal humiliation.

If I had any tears left, I might've started crying all over again.

Reluctantly and instinctively, I breathe in, and the taste of the moist, humid air makes me break into another coughing fit all over again.

I can feel the gentle support of a strong arm behind my back. A hand clumsily pushes my stringy hair away from my face, and I suddenly realize my so-called rescuer is holding me, but we have stopped moving. A second passes as he moves, and I suddenly find my legs dangling across his lap as he holds me against his chest.

"You'll be all right."

At the sound of the gentle reassurance in his voice, I am ready to scream.

I *didn't* want to be all right.

I *hadn't* wanted to be rescued.

But then I open my eyes, and our eyes meet.

Whoever my rescuer is, his eyes are a deep brown, the russet shadow cut through with amber strikes. My first clear thought is that he is not like any other man I've ever met; his skin is darker than mine, tanned by long hours in the open sun, the leather tunic he is wearing is thick. His arms are sturdy and his hair, even though it is as drenched as mine, is clearly darker than a starless night.

He isn't a grand beauty like Garrison, but there is something in his eyes that makes me feel strangely safe as we stare at each other.

His hand, covered by an archer's half-glove, reaches up and brushes against my cheek again, wiping away a small, wet leaf.

"I've got you." He speaks to me again, and this time, my ears pop, and I can hear the lower tenor of his voice more clearly. "Don't worry."

"Brenley? Brenley, where are you? Did you survive?"

The man holding me jerks his gaze away from me, as a woman's voice cuts through the waterfall's haze. I blink, taken aback by the sudden movement, until it dawns on me that the lady is calling for him.

"I'm over here," he calls back, and I can now safely infer his name is Brenley.

He looks down at me again. "Sorry," he said. "I know that was loud."

A small, reluctant smile tugs at my lips, a foreign sensation to me now, almost as foreign as my instinct to comfort others over myself. "It's all right."

My voice is soft and scratchy, but Brenley smiles and I find myself feeling even more strange as I look at him.

Why is he here? Who is he?

"Where did you say you were?" The woman's voice was back.

"He's over by the tidepool," another male voice replies, this one with a deeper bass to its sound.

"We're over here!" Brenley turns and hollers back, and that's when I see it.

There's an insignia on the cuff of his shoulder, just off to the side. From where I lay against him, I can just make out the markings.

It's a dragon with long, trailing wings, resting in a nest of fire.

Fuergo.

The mark of the Katorian Republic Armed Forces.

Garrison's enemy.

"No." I jolt back and let out a yelp as my forehead suddenly spikes with pain. I reach up to rub my temple, but my hand falls over his instead. I breathe in again and again, trying to reorient myself as I struggle to free myself from Brenley's arms.

"Stay still," he says, failing to realize my distress was due to him, and not anything else. "You fell down that waterfall and almost died, you know."

I know I almost died! I wanted to! I mentally scream at him, still trying to free myself from his arms.

"It'll be all right. I saved you." He holds onto me more tightly. "You're safe. You should try to rest."

At his words, I freeze, suddenly even more nauseated.

He saved my life.

Duty now demands my life is no longer my own—whoever this man is, I am now bound to him.

His other hand wraps around my wrist, and as a medic—*former medic*—I know he is checking for my pulse. I can feel the calluses on his fingers.

If I had more energy, I would've pushed him away, desperate to free myself.

But it is already too late. He has me in his arms, and with an impressive show of strength, he picks me up and begins hiking over the riverbank's rocks and sand, heading toward the woods.

I close my eyes.

What else can I do?

I'd tried to run away from my fate, but it's clear that I've failed.

"My friends are over here," Brenley tells me. "We don't have much, but we'll make sure you're taken care of, miss … ?"

He is asking for my name, and it is only duty that prompts me to answer him.

"Thessa," I whisper.

He pauses in his walk, and I open my eyes, only to see him staring down at me again.

"I'm Brenley." He introduces himself in a distracted manner, but he clears his throat a second later. "It's lovely to meet you, Thessa."

There's a whisper of reverence in his voice as he says my name, but all I can think of is Garrison. I close my eyes again and turn away from Brenley, hiding my face against his shoulder.

I am extremely grateful when Brenley continues walking. From his demeanor, he seems to think I am sick, and perhaps I am.

Heartsick.

I cannot cry any longer, even as my heart breaks all over again.

My forehead pounds with pain, and I beg for respite. Unconsciousness starts to claim me, and a small sigh escapes me.

The last thought I have as I fall away into darkness again is stark and clear and terrifying.

It was not supposed to be this way.

TO BE CONTINUED …

AUTHOR'S NOTE

Dear Reader,

My apologies always seem to both precede and follow these companion stories, and I feel compelled to uphold tradition in this case. *Dragon Tears* is a prequel novella to The Alliance of the Dragon Sword, a book series I have wanted to write for my husband for at least a good five years now.

I remember sitting down with him on our first date after we first became parents. We had family members watching our new son, and after the experience of childbirth and the birthing pains of learning how to parent, I only wanted to sit down with my husband and write a story with him. I am still to this day in awe of his love, and how much of our lives are entangled together because of it, as we can see with all our children now.

But at the time, I asked him to tell me what kind of book he would like, and so on and so forth, and so we began to discuss details. I've been amused over the years since then, about how we would talk of it, as I didn't like all of his ideas and he was appalled I would ask him to describe a story he'd like and I was objecting to it. He was the one who wanted the dragons and the higher-fantasy feel, and as my usual self, I wanted the characters and all their problems.

Now that it's been a while, and both parties are more reasonably settled, I have decided to set about writing the series, with the rest of the books in the series always further behind than I'd like. Thessa's character was important to me, because after having kids, I wanted to write a pregnant protagonist, and I especially wanted to write one to help crawl more into the shoes of Mary, the Mother of Jesus—but of course, I wanted to do it with a different twist to the story.

To me, especially as a mother, Mary is an aspiring figure—full of sweetness and faithfulness in the Biblical text. In my own pregnancies, I have thought about her and how she would willingly take on pregnancy and giving birth to the Son of God. Pregnancy was a learning experience for me, one that taught me just how selfish and little-longsuffering I can be. While it was also full of wonder and awe, I had cramps and contractions, stretchmarks and sleepy restlessness and so much more. After an experience, we tend to forget about the pain—which is why I have multiple children, I guess—but suffering for the sake of another, even my own little ones, was no easy battle, and as I came into this book and this series, I wanted to play with the question of "What if Mary had run away?" While I've clearly taken a little more imagination to it, I liked the idea of showing that love and suffering, and how it is both, as usual, a unique kind of pleasure and pain.

I also like the idea of giving Joseph more credit. He married into scandal and high stakes with a holy calling, and for a simple man who had been a carpenter, I imagine it was quite a shock. But despite the pressure around him and the hardship before him, he stayed, and he stayed faithful. That's nothing to take easily, or take for granted. I can well imagine Mary asking Joseph if he ever regretted staying beside her, especially if life is nothing like it was dreamt to be before.

I hope you'll join Thessa's story again in the first book in the series, *Call of the Dragon Sword*, coming not quite soon enough, when we get to see more of Brenley, the young man who saves Thessa, and the others who journey along with him.

Until We Meet Again,

C. S. Johnson

Thank you for reading! Please leave a review for this book and check out my other books for more adventures!

www.ingramcontent.com/pod-product-compliance
Lightning Source LLC
Chambersburg PA
CBHW030334310726
48979CB00001B/29

* 9 7 8 1 9 4 8 4 6 4 6 6 6 *